I0673576

Hot Crossed Buns

Spanking short stories:
erotic, play and discipline

Susan Kohler

CCB Publishing
British Columbia, Canada

Hot Crossed Buns: Spanking short stories: erotic, play and discipline

Copyright ©2007 by Susan Kohler
ISBN-13   978-0-9783893-2-1
First Edition

Library and Archives Canada Cataloguing in Publication

Kohler, Susan, 1950-
Hot Crossed Buns: Spanking short stories: erotic, play and discipline /
written by Susan Kohler. – 1st ed.
Also available in electronic format.
ISBN 978-0-9783893-2-1

1. Sexual dominance and submission--Fiction. 2. Sadomasochism--
Fiction. 3. Corporal punishment--Fiction. I. Title.
PS3611.O47H68 2007   813'.6   C2007-904209-0

Extreme care has been taken to ensure that all information presented in this
book is accurate and up to date at the time of publishing. Neither the author
nor the publisher can be held responsible for any errors or omissions.
Additionally, neither is any liability assumed for damages resulting from
the use of the information contained herein.

All rights reserved. No part of this publication may be reproduced, stored
in a retrieval system or transmitted in any form or by any means, electronic,
mechanical, photocopying, recording or otherwise without the express
written permission of the publisher.   Printed in the United States of
America and the United Kingdom.

Publisher: CCB Publishing
             British Columbia, Canada
             www.ccbpublishing.com

Dedication

This is dedicated to the man who warms my heart, and my bottom, and who sometimes allows me to warm his. He gave me a lot of ideas, love and encouragement. He kept me on my toes, or at least, not sitting down.

And also to Paul, who has worked so hard with me, and also given me so much of his time, knowledge and support.

Other books by Susan Kohler

The Paddle Club

Another Batch of Warm Buns

The Heart of the Beast

Preface

Call me weird, many do. I've always wanted to be spanked, not that my parents ever did. Besides, I've always wanted to be spanked by a lover. In other words, I wanted a sexual spanking long before I even knew such a thing existed.

Imagine my delight when I found literature that had sexual spankings on almost every page. Wow! But I soon got tired of the books I was finding that deal with spanking. Many were far too harsh, and made the women seem like victims, almost as if their only purpose was to give the spanker a bottom to spank. Most of them had no fun in them. Bummer! They were also, for the most part, either set in the past or in a foreign land. I wanted an updated, upbeat collection of stories with men I would like to be involved with, and women I would like to know.

Finally I found a lover who loves to spank me and sometimes for me to spank him. I let him talk me into trying spanking. To this day, he thinks it was his idea. I was in Heaven!

I had been writing some stories for him, so I put them together and wound up with a book of short stories. Imagine my shock when some of those stories got together, seemingly all on their own, and formed a novel. Eventually, I had two sets of short stories, and one full length spanking novel.

In my stories, some of the spankings are just for fun, and some are for discipline. All sex is voluntary. Also, sometimes the one getting spanked is a man. I have found that many men are bottoms, or like to switch, but most stories are male spanks female or female spanks female.

I put comments in front of each story, and at the end. In some ways these comments are my favorite parts to write. I feel like I'm chatting with a friend. Feel free to skip the comments if you'd like.

Also, please remember that not everyone harbors a secret desire to be whipped or spanked, I just left anyone who doesn't out of this book.

All right everyone, drop your pants and bend over. Let the spanking begin!

Contents

HOT CROSSED BUNS

One

Store Bought Pain

The story of what happens to a woman who has fantasized for years about being spanked, about how she felt intrigued by the idea of making her fantasy a reality. She soon learned that sometimes when you hire a faceless stranger to bring your secret fantasies to life, you can get much more than you bargain for.

Sarah didn't know where the fantasy had first come from or how it had taken such a powerful hold on her, but as far back as she could even remember she had quite often fantasized about being spanked and whipped. She had fantasies about it almost daily. She would get aroused thinking about a man ordering her to lower her panties, commanding her to place herself across his knees. She almost came before she got to the part where she pictured his large hand descending onto her bare bottom with a resounding crack!

It was much more than a fantasy. She had a real desire to be spanked, and had always found literature with spanking scenes very arousing. Even when the spankings they wrote about were very extreme. Far too extreme for her to want in real life.

Mind you, she had never been spanked in real life. In what she thought of as her rational self she thought that anyone who wanted a spanking, a hard spanking, was more than a little sick. Rationally, she thought that a man who enjoyed spanking a woman was abusive. Rationally, she was afraid of the loss of control and of the pain. Emotionally, however, she longed for a good hard spanking.

She did not know why this fantasy turned her on. She was not attracted to the idea of pain. To the contrary, she was terrified at the very thought of the sting that a spanking would bring. She always had been afraid of physical pain.

She was also sure she would die of nerves and embarrassment as she lowered her panties for the spanking. She could not even imagine standing in front of a man and preparing for him to punish her. She told herself that she must be sick or crazy but she desperately wanted the naughty daydreams to become a painful reality.

In her favorite version of the fantasy, she went to a man, a complete stranger, and asked him, no, begged him, to give her a severe spanking. She didn't want him to degrade her or order her around. He was not supposed to act mean or abusive in any way, except for the very tangible act of spanking her. He would be kind and considerate, but his manner would also be very firm and commanding. The man of her fantasy was nameless, faceless and almost unimportant, except as the means to her punishment.

She would humbly ask the man for the spanking and when she got it, if it wasn't harsh enough, she would quietly ask to be spanked again. The second time he would do it more severely, sometimes not just with his hand, but with a paddle or a whip.

Once in a while, in her fantasy, there was a form of role reversal as a follow-up. In these fantasies, after punishing her, the man became a sort of sex slave who would do anything she wanted. He would go to any extent possible to give her pleasure.

The fantasy had never happened to her and she was starting to feel an almost desperate urge for it. The spanking fantasy was all she thought about. It had become an obsession. Was she sick? She didn't think so; she had heard it was a fairly common fantasy. She read a lot of books like *The Pearl* and *The Story of O.*

The problem was, how could she get a spanking? The one thing she had never done, couldn't have done, was tell her lover what she wanted. She didn't have a lover; in fact, she had never had a lover she trusted enough to share this particular fantasy with. She had never had someone who really cared about what she wanted, her former lovers had only seemed to care about satisfying their own needs.

She was an attractive young woman; lively and good company so she dated often, of course, but there was no one she could allow herself to share her secret desires with. She kept her desire hidden like a shameful secret. Even though as a part of her fantasy she was supposed to be the one to bring up the subject, Sarah was very timid.

She wanted to ask for the spanking, but she was too shy. What she really wanted was for an unknown tormentor who would actually compel her to ask explicitly for a spanking. Still, she couldn't get up enough nerve to force herself to bring the subject up with any of her dates.

What if she brought it up and the man thought she was sick? Perverted? Even more troubling, what if he agreed to do it? Would she like it? If she did not like it, would he stop at her word?

One day she found a discarded underground paper. She found most of the articles a little sick and disgusting. The personal ads, however, were eye openers. There were pages and pages of ads from men and women offering to spank someone or to be spanked. Sometimes the ads were just a way to meet like-minded partners, and sometimes the ads were placed by people who spanked for money.

Sarah finally decided to hire someone to give her the fantasy. She felt that someone who advertised in the adult personals would understand her desire, or at least not judge her for having that desire. She also had a deep-seated feeling that if she paid for the spanking her tormentor would really be just a faceless stranger, and she would actually be the one in control. The man she hired would do just what she wanted, in the way she wanted it done.

Sarah was in for the surprise of her life.

She got a newer copy of an underground singles' newspaper that always carried suggestive ads, and then called the ones that mentioned discipline, or correction, or submission. She talked to several people, both men and women. The women were really helpful; they offered her advice and made her realize how prevalent her secret desires were, but for some reason she wanted to be spanked by a man. Several of the women mentioned a name and gave her a phone number. She didn't see an ad from this man, but made sure she kept his number. After all, he had references for being safe and following the woman's lead.

Before calling him, she talked to a few more men from the paper. She tried to describe the scene she wanted, but she felt uncomfortable speaking to most of the men. None of them seemed quite right to her until she gave up and called the person whose name and number she got from several women. A man named Mac.

On the phone, Mac sounded friendly, cheerful and surprisingly normal. He seemed very open. He listened to what she said she wanted, how she wanted him to treat her, and how severe she wanted him to be. He had some suggestions but he listened to her desires and his suggestions were designed to enhance her ideal scene, not to change it.

He seemed perfectly understanding and agreeable to everything she said. She felt he would give her the precise fantasy she wanted, and in just the way she wanted it. She knew because of the references that she would be safe, and he would stop if she wanted him to.

He said he had his garage set up just for spanking scenes. It was not a dungeon, just a really comfortable, soundproof room. He quoted her a reasonable price, and gently suggested a date and time. She made an appointment with him.

It was even better for Sarah to realize that he wanted to be paid for spanking her because he would have no personal stake in the fantasy, except to please her.

According to their agreement, there was to be no actual sex involved, just the spanking and the feeling of helplessness and submission that comes from being at the mercy of a stranger who would punish her without feelings, with no sympathy or compunction, but also without degradation.

Sarah stood on the sidewalk with her legs shaking for a long time before she gathered her courage and walked up the gravel driveway at the address she had gotten from the voice on the phone. In her right hand was a riding crop that she had bought just for tonight, just for this still faceless stranger to use on her butt. It felt like it weighed a ton, and it was just too long to hide. She hoped none of his neighbors saw it. She flushed, thinking to herself of how it had felt to go into a saddle shop and buy it. She had been sure everyone in the shop knew why she was buying the crop, knew she wasn't ever going to use it on a horse.

She walked to the garage as Mac had instructed her to. Mac had been more than willing to go to Sarah, but he knew instinctively that part of her fantasy was to bring herself to him, to request the spanking. She remembered him telling her that the garage had been converted into a special room, just for one purpose: to accommodate women like herself. Women who wanted to be spanked.

She arrived at his door at exactly 8 pm, the appointed time. He had warned her that there would be a penalty if she was late. As much as she wanted a spanking, she wasn't sure she wanted a penalty, whatever it would be. She rang the doorbell and waited.

As she stood at the door, she felt like her whole body was tingling with fear and anticipation, especially her backside. Her mouth was dry, and she felt shivers running down her spine. She waited, hardly knowing that what was behind the door would change her whole life. Forever.

When he opened the door, the first thing she noticed was that the man she had hired was gorgeous. If she had ordered her ideal man from a catalog, he would look just like the man standing before her. He had dark wavy hair, bright blue eyes, a magnificent body with a muscular build and a great smile. He was dressed in tan slacks and a blue and white knit sweater that set off his eyes perfectly.

"Hi," he said, in a relaxed and friendly voice. He had the most friendly, open smile Sarah had ever seen. He also had a hint of humor in his face.

"I'm Mac, you must be Sarah?" At her nervous nod, he said,

"Come in. I won't hurt you," he paused and flashed her another smile, full of the devil and good humor, "much. Trust me. You're right on time. I'm disappointed."

Sarah found her voice. "Why?" she asked, entering the room.

He held the door to the room wide open, and looking inside, she could see that it was warm and cozy, furnished like any ordinary bedroom. It had a large four poster bed and a dresser, both in walnut. The room had a closet, a bathroom and even a small refrigerator. The walls were painted a pale blue, and the bedspread was royal blue. He had told her over the phone that the room was completely soundproofed.

"So you can scream all you want." She remembered that he had laughed with genuine good humor when he told her that, but Sarah still felt another race of shivers run down her spine.

He shut the door behind her and locked it with a loud click, bringing her back to the present and stopping her memories cold in their tracks.

"I promised you a penalty for being late," he said softly. "Maybe I should give you a penalty for disappointing me," he whispered in her ear.

"That hardly seems fair!" It was a weak protest.

"Sarah, my sweet, I've been known to spank women for just breathing. How is that fair?" He smiled at her, then flashed her a stern look. "So? Why were you not late?"

"I'm sorry, I was too scared to be late," Sarah whispered.

"Silly girl," Mac chided, "come here."

She entered the room and walked right into his arms. His hug was warm and friendly. His large, gentle hands were sliding up and down her back and slowly made their way down to her ass. He raised the dress she was wearing without breaking off the hug, still reaching around her. He gave her several hard, sharp slaps on her behind. He slid his hands inside her underwear taking one cheek in each hand and squeezing it gently. He slid his hands out of her panties and gave her ass a couple of more sharp slaps. To Sarah the slaps were stinging and felt great, but they were not enough. She wanted more. Finally he released her from the hug and stepped away from her.

He looked at her expectantly. "Okay, Sarah, what do you want?" he asked gently with his soft, deep voice.

It was finally happening. Her fantasy was about to begin. Some of the things she had discussed with him on the phone were the Victorian novels she had read. In the books, the girls were always made to ask for their punishment in very explicit and humiliating ways. Now it was her turn. She froze.

"I want you to give me a good hard spanking." Her voice was a soft shy whisper; her face was warm with a blush.

Mac prodded her, his voice soft but still firm, "Sarah?"

"I'm torn, I want to run and I want to stay," she admitted in a soft voice.

Mac had an uncanny instinct about these things so he asked her quietly, "How will you feel if you leave now? After coming this far?"

"Very smart," Sarah smiled, her humor returning, "and painless, and... "

"Like a coward?" Mac supplied.

"Yes," she admitted, "like a coward, and still curious, and embarrassed."

"Never feel embarrassed around me, Sarah dear, I'm not judging you," Mac smiled. "I think you're judging yourself. I do think, however, that if you leave you'll regret it, and you'll punish yourself for it. I think you'll be even harder on yourself than I ever could be. So tell me Sarah," he took on a harder tone, "what do you want?"

She bit at her lip, then shot him a pleading look with her big green eyes. "Please, Mac, give me a spanking."

Her voice sounded small, her throat was tight and dry.

"A spanking?" he asked gently, seeming to consider the idea. "Hard?"

She nodded, her short red curls bouncing, and then she found her voice, "Hard."

She moved quickly to do as he requested.

"Bare bottom?" he prodded, drawing her out.

"Yes," she barely made any sound.

"Yes, what? Say it, girl, and speak up!" He was firmer, more masterful.

"Bare bottom." It came out louder.

"Please," he prompted.

"Please," she nodded, sounding terrified, sounding thrilled.

"Across my lap?" he questioned.

"Yes, please, across your lap," she replied, with her head hanging down.

"With my hand?" he asked firmly, still leading her. "Say all of it, again."

She took a deep breath and met his gaze. "Mac, would you please give me a very long, hard spanking with your hand on my bare bottom, while I lay face down across your knees? Please?"

"Of course, my dear. I'll give you as good a spanking as I ever gave anyone. I'll set your lovely ass on fire for you. I'll make it turn a very bright red and I'll make it sting like the devil. I promise." Suddenly Mac barked out an order, "Come here, now!"

His tone left no room for hesitation. Sarah did as she was told. Following his orders, she moved the plain wooden chair into the center of the small room.

"I want plenty of room to raise my arm when I spank you," Mac said watching her carefully, judging her reactions.

She moved the chair into place. He stood there, watching her. "Now, push up the right sleeve of my sweater for me," he ordered, "and kiss the palm of my right hand. The hand I'm going to use to spank you very hard."

She reached out and pushed up his sleeve. She slowly slid her hand down to his hand and kissed the rough palm.

After the required kiss, he sat in the straight-backed chair and patted his lap. "Over my knees, now. Sweet Sarah. It's time."

Feeling awkward, Sarah draped herself across his knees. Mac spanked her without even raising her skirt. It was not a hard spanking, just playful and teasing. It was just a little harder than the swats he'd given her while hugging her. Sarah was almost

16

disappointed when suddenly Mac began to pick up the pace of the blows. They weren't really harder, just faster, but they began to sting.

Suddenly, without a word, Mac raised Sarah's skirt up and began spanking her on her lacy blue panties. He began to put more slap into it, stinging but without real force. Sarah's bottom began to tingle.

Mac stopped again. He stroked and admired her slightly pink bottom, gently patting it and even bending down to kiss and nip it

"Now Sarah, your spanking will begin," Mac said. "Stand up, remove your dress and hang it in the closet."

She quickly removed her floral print summer dress, hanging it neatly in the closet, stepped out of her shoes then pulled off her pantyhose. She produced two long scarves from her purse.

She walked over to face him, wearing only her matching panties and bra, and placed the scarves in his open palm. She gingerly laid herself over his lap. She reached back to lower her lacy blue nylon panties, but Mac stopped her. Mac used one scarf and tied her hands together, and she had an instant feeling of helplessness. With the second scarf he tied both hands to the chair leg.

When she was finally tied in place, she almost fainted from her feelings of excitement and panic. Feelings that only increased when she felt Mac gently lower her lacy panties, so that they hung on her legs, down almost to her knees.

Mac spent a long time fondling her buttocks gently. Rubbing small soft circles over the area that would soon received the punishment. He even planted a kiss and a nip on her firm round butt! Sarah squirmed in an agony of nervous anticipation.

"Stop squirming!" he commanded sternly.

"The suspense is killing me!" Sarah moaned.

"Gee. That's too bad." Mac's sympathy was obviously false. "I'll have to end the suspense then."

Without warning, he exploded with a series of hard, fast slaps on her butt. Each of the slaps made a loud sound in the small room. Crack! The blows landed first on one cheek and then the other, turning her delicate pink skin red, very red, and making Sarah yell out loud and squirm.

"Lay still, girl, and relax your ass or it will be all the harder on you!" There was no gentleness now, no soft voice, just a firm, strong command.

Somehow, Sarah forced herself to obey. Crack! The spanking began again, but this time it was not quite so hard, not coming quite so fast. As her bottom warmed up, the speed and intensity of the spanking built up. It went on and on. He built up the force and speed of the spanking, then lowered it only to start building the intensity up again.

Sarah's ass was on fire, and the pain was excruciating and thrilling. Finally, after what seemed like forever, he quit spanking her.

He did not untie her right away. First, he rubbed some cool lotion on her throbbing bottom, then, judging her reactions, he pulled the cheeks apart and lightly fingered her clit and her anus. He was ready to stop at any sign of resistance to this treatment; after all, it was not part of what they had planned. Sarah seemed to relax and revel in his touch. So he gave her a few moments of gentle teasing.

He untied her hands and had her stand in front of him, facing away from him. He sat there looking at her buttocks, admiring the color he had put on them.

He stood up. "Sarah, put the chair back where you found it, and then stand in the corner with your panties down until I tell you to move." He watched as she complied. "And do not even think about rubbing your bottom!"

"Now you must thank me for giving you such a good, hard spanking, and turning your lovely ass such a nice, bright red," he commanded after she had stood in the corner for a few minutes.

"Th… thank you for the good, hard spanking," she whispered, turning her head and looking over her shoulder at him. She was quite a sight, her face almost as red as her hair, or her butt. "And for turning my ass so red."

He reached out and carefully pulled her dainty underwear back into place, then gently turned her around and pulled her into his arms and briefly cuddled her before telling her to put her face back in the corner and wait for more orders.

Mac moved away from her and sat in his massive, padded armchair. He watched Sarah and used his instincts, which were incredible, to gauge whether Sarah would want to take this farther.

All his years of experience told him she was a true find. She would take all he could give and enjoy it; she just didn't know it yet. She was also very sweet and very pretty.

Mac admitted to himself that for the first time in his life he was seriously attracted to a paying customer.

"Sweet Sarah, come over here and sit on my lap," Mac said softly. As she approached, he pulled her down onto his lap.

He hugged her gently and stroked her hair. She settled into his arms with a contented sigh, her head resting on his chest, just under his chin. They sat like that for a long time, talking softly and just relaxing.

After about half an hour or so, Mac said softly, "Sarah, did I tell you there's something I never do?"

"No, I can't think of anything," she said softly, looking up at him. "Unless it was that you never have sex with your clients, or even kiss them."

"That's the thing I was thinking of, the kiss, not the sex," he said. "I never do either one with a client, but right now I was thinking about how I never kiss a client, ever."

"And you're telling me this because?" she asked him, her eyes wide and questioning.

"Because of this." He kissed her; a long tender kiss, starting soft and romantic and quickly building intensity. The kiss never slid over into the realm of full on passion but it was warm and sweet, with a hint of the fire to come.

Sarah found her voice, "I'm glad you cleared that up."

She continued to sit, perched precariously on his knee for a very long time. He whispered soft endearments in her ear and comforted her for a very long time. She gloried in the cuddling and the comforting warmth of his arms around her. Eventually he told her to stand in front of him again.

"Now, girl, it's time to move ahead. Tell me what else you want me to do to you." His voice was firm and commanding again.

This time she answered him more easily, "I want you to whip me, using the riding crop that I brought along, on my bare butt and make it very, very hard, please."

She stood quietly in front of him, with her hands folded like a good little girl, feeling more than a little stunned. Surprised at how easily she asked for a whipping. Her buttocks still throbbed from the spanking but the sharp pain had faded.

He had untied her hands from the chair leg, and untied one hand, but there was still a knot around the wrist of the other.

"Okay, Sarah girl, remove your underwear completely and go stand at the end of the bed," he ordered.

There was a cedar hope chest at the foot of the four-poster bed, so Sarah was really standing about three feet away from the bed. Mac had her stand halfway between the two bedposts, and then he pulled her forward and tied the wrist with the scarf attached to it to one post. He tied the other wrist to the other post the same way. Because of the chest she was bent slightly forward with her buttocks pushed out. It was an uncomfortable and humiliating position. Sarah could move her feet and wiggle her behind, but her tied hands kept her partially immobilized. Mac startled her by tying a blindfold over her face then he told her he was going to relax for a while, and that she would have to wait a few minutes for her whipping!

"You don't mind waiting, do you little girl?" he asked harshly.

"Please Mac, whip me now. Please don't make me wait." Sarah was shaking.

"You'll regret that remark when I do get around to whipping you," Mac said sternly. "You'll wish I'd made the wait longer."

She was both eager and frightened half out of her mind; the waiting and the blindfold only heightened her tension. Her emotions were heightened, her nerves on a razor's edge.

20

That was the point, of course. That, and to let any traces of pain from the spanking settle in a little. Mac decided to make this memorable for Sarah and for himself. For once it wasn't just business, a way to earn a little extra income. He was entranced by Sarah. She was the most beautiful, sweetest, and least jaded woman he'd seen in a long time. She was very brave too. I'm in trouble, he thought. A client no less, who would have guessed? He decided to take this a lot farther than their original agreement. She had a few surprises in store for her, both before and after the whipping with her new riding crop.

In time Sarah began to fidget and whimper a little, and Mac worried that he'd pushed too hard. After all, this was the first time she'd played any spanking games.

"Too scared to carry on, little one?" he asked being deliberately sarcastic. "Going to chicken out?"

Sarah couldn't answer, couldn't even nod, which suited Mac just fine. He picked up the crop and began to swish it through the air, making Sarah flinch before he ever brought it down on her trembling butt. He walked around behind her and Sarah tensed, waiting for the slash of pain. She waited for nothing; he didn't bring the crop down on her ass right away, but set it on the hope chest beside her, then pulled a chair up behind her and sat down.

Sarah was scared and puzzled.

"What are you doing?" she questioned.

Mac replied, "I just thought I'd have a little extra fun before using the riding crop. This is nothing compared to what I'm planning to do between the riding crop and your third whipping!"

"Third whipping!" she sputtered. "But, but this is all I paid for, it's as far as I wanted it to go. You can't!" she protested. "What are you doing now?"

"Hey girl, remember you're tied up! I can, and I will do whatever I want to you." He leaned over and gently nipped her still hot pink butt. His voice became gentler as he added in a softly persuading tone, "Relax baby, you'll love it. I also want you to know that this has nothing to do with money, this is just for fun between us. Trust me, you have so far."

She gave him a faint nod. He placed his hands on each side of her ass, lowered his head and began to kiss and tease her ass. He took more little nips of her butt, and used his tongue on the tight opening of her anus, sliding the fingers of one hand into her vagina. Sarah squirmed and wiggled as she became more and more aroused. Still he continued, working his magic with his tongue and teeth. Before long, she came.

As soon as she stopped shivering with the force of her orgasm, Mac got on with the original business. He picked up the crop and brought it slashing down on her buttocks. He gave her a harsh whipping, but not so severe that it did any real damage; he didn't leave any deep bruises or welts. Her butt was even redder now than before and it hurt terribly. When he was done, he untied Sarah's hands and pushed the blanket chest off to one side. He had Sarah sit on the hard wooden chest, ignoring her sore bottom.

He told her to remove her blindfold. There were traces of tears in her green eyes, making them sparkle like emeralds, and a soft shy smile on her trembling lips.

After a while, Mac told her to remove her bra and then sit on the end of the bed; then to lie back, with her legs hanging off the end of the bed. She blushed as she removed her bra but she complied without protest.

He moved quickly, before Sarah could react. Using the restraints that he kept in place on the bedposts at the front of the bed, he retied Sarah with her arms up over her head. He pulled the chair back to the end of the bed and lowered his mouth almost down to her hot cunt.

He looked up at her with one eyebrow cocked, "Okay?"

When she raised her head up and nodded, speechless, he lowered his mouth. He ate her out with his skillful tongue until she came again, then he moved up to her firm, round breasts. He suckled and kissed her breasts for a long time.

He climbed upon the bed, kneeling with one knee on each side of her hips. Using his hands to push her breasts together, he pushed his large prick in and out of the valley between them. He fucked her cleavage until he was almost to the point of orgasm. He climbed farther up on the bed still straddling her, until he had his erect cock very near her face.

"I thought our plan was for no sex," she laughed, teasing.

"I came up with a new plan," he told her seriously.

"Don't tell me," she smiled, "let me guess."

She raised her head again and immediately took his prick into her sweet mouth, sucking and licking, and somehow humming at the same time. Mac caught his breath as he recognized the tune. It was the popular theme from a movie about sharks. He froze for a moment.

Sarah stopped what she was doing just long enough to look up at him with a sly grin and say, "Trust me!"

Mac laughed even as he shot his load of cum deep into her throat. They lay there together as they recovered. Eventually he began to tease her a bit, arousing both of them again.

"Okay. What's next, fucking or sodomy?" he asked, only half joking, lazily stroking her still red butt.

Her reply was soft and serious. "I've never tried, uh, sodomy before."

"So okay, we'll fuck and save sodomy for the grand finale," he said rolling over on top of her. "After the last whipping."

"There's going to be more?" she asked amazed.

"There's going to be lots more," he replied, solemnly.

"Can I have my hands free?" Sarah requested softly.

"Not yet, love." He kissed her nose.

At that point as he entered her cunt, she wasn't about to argue with anything. They rocked and thrashed together in a primal frenzy until the explosive climax came, shocking them both in its intensity. Sarah had never been tied up during sex before, and she discovered that it added an extra spice, an out-of-control feeling to the sensuality of the experience. Especially since her buttocks still ached and throbbed from the harsh punishment they had received at Mac's hand.

Once again they rested; Mac opened a bottle of champagne and held the glass while Sarah drank. Although her arms were beginning to ache, she did not ask again to be set free.

Mac untied her eventually, though. He held her and stroked her, treating her so gently that she could scarcely believe he had just whipped her mercilessly with a riding crop and spanked her bare ass savagely with his hands.

How it happened, she never really knew, but suddenly she was on her belly again, her hands tied to the headboards again. She was bent over the end of the bed, her feet on the floor. Mac fastened her feet to the legs of the bed. He got out his camera and began to take pictures of her. He photographed her red behind, her welts, her cunt, everything he could focus on. She started to protest then she laughed as she heard the already familiar phrase.

"Trust me!"

He set the camera up on a tripod, then went over to the closet and brought out a big birch rod, shaking it to loosen it up. It whistled as he swished it through the air. Sarah noticed that a few drops of moisture sprinkled off the rod as he flicked it lightly.

He showed it to Sarah. "It's a real birch rod with all the buds on it, and it has been soaked in brine. It should hurt quite a lot, maybe it'll even cut you, does that sound okay?"

Sarah felt hypnotized at the sight and sound of the rod, fascinated and slightly sick, but still she nodded and replied quietly, "I trust you."

"Then ask me to birch you, ask me really nice," he said.

"Please sir, birch my bare bottom as hard as you can," she swallowed, "please."

"Girl, I'll whip you until the blood runs down your legs and you can't sit down or lay flat on your back for a week." By now Sarah knew Mac well enough to be sure that it was a gross exaggeration, meant to titillate her.

Mac focused the camera on Sarah's ass and used a remote button to snap pictures of the rod hitting her behind. After a few pictures, he put down the remote and concentrated on whipping her.

It wasn't severe as birchings go but he still used the rod hard enough to raise a few faint welts and even cause a few drops of blood. He finished off with half a dozen cuts, harder than the rest. Then he stopped and took a few more pictures.

"It's time to thank me, little girl," Mac said sternly.

"Thank you for the whipping," Sarah murmured, sounding like she didn't have much energy left. This time there were more than traces of tears in her lovely eyes. This time she had tears running down her face and she was fighting herself to keep from sobbing openly.

He untied her and ordered her to kiss the rod and put it away. When she had done as ordered, he had her get back into the position, and tied her to the bed again. He took out some lubricating cream which he spread on her anus, on his fingers and on his cock. Then he gently began to finger fuck her anus; taking his time he worked one, then two, and finally three fingers into her asshole.

When she was ready he inserted his prick into her anus, and gently began to move within her as she relaxed and opened herself up, enjoying the sensations that he was giving her. She even enjoyed the feeling of him ramming up against her painful buttocks. He pumped her harder and harder. He managed to grab the button for the camera and snap a few pictures of his cock in her ass before throwing it aside and building up to a frantic climax.

He helped her lay face down on the bed and gently bathed and treated her sore bottom. Before she could ask what he was going to do with the pictures, he gave her the roll of film.

"A souvenir of what I hope is not our only night together, and I don't mean to say that I want you for a regular client! I really want you in my life, Sarah, love. I think I might even want you in my business too." He paused, kissing her gently. "Do you think you could give a whipping as well as you can take one?"

Sarah gave him a devilish grin. "I'd be glad to demonstrate any time. You deserve a little payback."

"Somehow I think I'll wait until you cool down, and I don't just mean your behind, before I let you anywhere near my butt." He kissed her on the end of the nose. "I am a very wise man."

"Did you say you were a wise man," she said with a sly grin, "or a wise ass?"

"Just insult me, why don't you? Just when I was going to be nice and give you your money back." He handed her the money and became serious. "What we had tonight was more than a just little spanking. It was really great between us, and more than just wild, kinky sex. If I kept your money I'd feel like a prostitute, and even more important, you would think of me as one. The sex we had was something special, not just part of a deal."

Sarah took the money and the roll of film. She said, "Oh my God! First, I think you're very special too. We're special together. I would like to be with you in any way, at any time," she laughed. "Second, how on earth do I get this film developed? It's probably just a little too sexy for the drug store."

"I don't know what you mean," he teased. "It's only sodomy and S & M, what's so sexy about that?"

"If you don't know, you're doing it wrong," she needled him. "I know I'm not going to hand this to the guy at the Photo counter."

"Don't worry, I have a darkroom, but I didn't want you to have any anxiety about my having the negatives to do anything weird with them." He grinned, "If you want, we can develop them together."

"Mac, my dear," she rolled over, ignoring the pain in her buttocks, and reached up for him, "I'd love to spend time in a dark room, any dark room with you, anytime." She pulled him down to her, and slid one hand down to gently stroke him. "Are you in any hurry to develop that film?"

"No, Sarah, love," he entered her, "let's see what we can develop right here."

I did all this in one sitting, but I'm a little surprised that I can even sit. My lover beat my butt, good and hard, just for research. Damn good of him, wasn't it? He also offered to tie me up and sodomize me, again in the name of research. I'll keep it in mind!

Two

I'd Rather Face The Judge

If a wife is careless with her husband's most precious possession, how angry will he be? And what if she herself is that most precious possession? Does he take her punishment to a level that even leaves him shaken?

Linda and Fred had been married for about five years, and they were very happy years. Fred made a good living, and so did Linda. They weren't rich by any means, but they were comfortable. They didn't have any children yet, but they were looking forward to having one fairly soon.

They were an attractive couple. Fred had salt and pepper hair, a little surprising at his age, but the color really set off his slate blue eyes. His eyes should have seemed cold, but they seldom were. He was an easygoing man, filled with enough life and joy that his eyes sparkled with warmth. Linda had more curves than was fashionable but they looked great on her. Her hair was warm sable, and her hazel eyes were always filled with amusement. Almost always.

Linda and Fred played spanking games, just for fun. It was simply a part of their love play. It was teasing and fun, lighthearted, and never taken to extremes. The only time it was more serious was when Fred gave Linda a discipline spanking.

However he seldom did that. Fred had several reasons for not using domestic discipline very often. For one thing, he preferred to have spanking as a part of their fun play, and he felt that too many discipline spankings would take the fun out of it. For another, he believed that for him to use discipline on Linda meant he had to be practically perfect, and he knew he was a long ways from it. He was also a very kind man at heart and very much in love with Linda.

Fred would never spank Linda for spending too much money, for instance, or for talking back to him. He didn't care if she swore like a drunken sailor. He never lectured her about her manners or how she dressed. He never got angry if she argued with him or acted defiant. The only two things he would discipline her for were doing something to put herself in danger, and lying about it.

If she did something careless or unsafe, and if she took a risk of hurting herself or others, he would step in and he would be merciless. He wanted her with him for a long, long time. That didn't mean she couldn't play sports, ride horses or go out with the girls. It just meant she had to do things with safety in mind, avoiding unnecessary risks. Things like wearing a helmet when she rode her bike, or calling him if she got stranded somewhere and felt unsafe. Even calling him if she had a few drinks, instead of driving home.

Of course lying to avoid chastisement was also a big blunder; if she were caught, she would get double the punishment. It was worse, far worse, and he often threatened that it would be repeated the next day. So far, it never had.

Linda was in the kitchen fixing dinner, when Fred started balancing the checkbook and paying the monthly bills. He looked in her purse like he always did, looking for her checkbook and the log she kept of ATM withdrawals and debit purchases. He went through the bills, which were set aside for payment, and checked the day's mail for any new bills and credit card statements. He saw an envelope from the court system and put it in the stack, thinking it was probably jury duty. He spread it all out on his desk, sorting things into neat little piles.

He opened the letter and his blood ran cold. Linda had gotten a speeding ticket, one of the few things guaranteed to earn her a serious spanking. The fact that she hadn't told him about it only made it worse. The fact that is was for going twenty miles over the limit, sealed her fate. Twenty miles! What did she think she was doing, re-enacting the Indianapolis 500?

He set the incriminating letter aside and went back to the checkbook. He deducted all the ATM withdrawals each of them had made, and the debit purchases, and looked over the checks, totaling everything. He was so engrossed in the math, he almost missed the realization of one entry in her checkbook.

He looked over the batch of cancelled checks the bank had enclosed with the statement. His blood began to boil. There was another fine paid to the court system. A large fine. He checked the date, and sure enough – it was paid before Linda got the speeding ticket. That meant she had two tickets in one month and hadn't told him about either one. Her goose was well and truly cooked.

Linda peaked out of the kitchen and saw Fred with the checkbook from her purse. She knew he would find the check for the ticket she'd paid. She wondered if she could come up with any reason for paying that big a fine that would not get her spanked. Or, if she did find a suitable explanation, would she be able to get Fred to believe her.

She knew if she didn't find a way out of it, she was in trouble big time. He would consider it two things to be punished: for the ticket, and not telling him up front. She didn't mind spanking but Fred's discipline spankings were well, a pain in the ass.

"Fred, I have dinner ready," she said sounding as if she didn't have a care in the world.

She walked over to him and slipped her arms around his neck. As she looked down at the desk, she saw the envelope. It looked so familiar, just like the one she got telling her how much it was going to cost her for her last speeding ticket. It was opened, but the contents were still inside the envelope. Maybe he hadn't pulled them out and read it yet, she hoped. Somehow, she knew she wasn't going to be that lucky.

Fred turned his head and kissed her. "I'll be right there, love," he said, not seeming to have anything on his mind. "You wouldn't believe how high our insurance is going up! It's criminal! We're safe drivers. We don't have any accidents or tickets on our records."

"It's terrible, I know," she said faintly, as she went back to the kitchen.

They had a pleasant meal. She had prepared a casserole and a salad. There was a fresh strawberry pie, which he had brought home for dessert. They talked about their day over dinner. He never let her know that he had seen the tickets.

They watched a little TV, sitting side by side on the sofa, before going up to bed. As they got ready for bed, he got amorous. He was kissing her and teasing her, arousing her.

She got a spanking all right, fun and erotic, followed by a bout of lovemaking that, well, topped the chart of what they've had recently. They made love so tenderly and passionately that it seemed like the first fire of their romance. Afterwards, as she cuddled in his arms, she thought she'd been lucky. Apparently he hadn't noticed the speeding tickets.

She began to drift off to sleep, contented and sated. She barely felt him get out of bed. She never realized that he had pulled on his jeans and a T-shirt. Nothing fazed her until he shook her awake.

"Linda, wake up!" he commanded. "And I mean now!"

"Fred, what is it?" She yawned and stretched.

"It's time for you to pay for your speeding tickets," he said sternly, "and for not telling me about them in the first place. Did you think you could hide them from me? Did you think I wouldn't notice? Get in the corner."

Linda sat up, instantly awake, and instantly dreading what she knew was coming. "I'm sorry," she whispered, knowing it wouldn't help her at all. She was shaking as she stood up and walked into the corner. She hated corner time, but she hated what came after even more.

He went to their collection of toys and began to search through, considering and rejecting some, pulling others out. He had a paddle, a strap and the cane laid out before he told her to come over to the bed.

He was sitting on the edge of the bed, and he sternly ordered her to stand in front of him, with her eyes down. In spite of that she noticed he had pulled out the most stinging paddle and strap, not the ones that caused the most deep tissue pain. She puzzled at that even as he began the lecture. And it was some lecture.

"Linda, I love you," he began, "and my biggest fear is losing you. I don't know how I'd cope, how I'd even go on if anything happened to you. That's why the only time I really get mad is when you take unnecessary risks. Risks like drinking and driving, or driving after having a few drinks, or in bad weather. You can call me anytime and we'll work out a way for you to get home safely."

"You can call a cab or find a safe place to stay overnight. Whatever it takes. I do the same thing because I never want to leave you."

"I'm so sorry," she said simply, her head hung low.

"I know you are," he told her quietly, "but speeding is something you can avoid. Just slow down. There is no place you have to be so bad that you can't take time to get there safely. I lost two family members and one friend to traffic accidents. Do you think I want to lose you too?"

"No, Fred."

"You were going 20 miles over the speed limit, or more, when you got one ticket. How fast were you going when you got the other?"

"It was written as 45 in a 30 MPH zone," she admitted softly, "but it was more like 50."

"So you need to learn a lesson, a very serious lesson," he said firmly. "You need to learn to follow the posted speed limits. Do you agree?"

"Yes, Fred."

"And you need to learn this lesson twice over, agreed?"

"Yes, Fred."

"There's something more," he glared at her, "I hate it when you lie to me. It's the only other thing I get mad about."

"I didn..." she began.

"By not telling me and accepting your punishment, that's just what you did." There was no compromise in his voice. None in his eyes. "You will pay for those lies as well as the two tickets. I'm afraid it will take more than I can give you in one night. You will be punished tonight and again tomorrow night. Tonight we'll use the stinging implements, and tomorrow we'll use the ones that go deeper."

"Fred." It sounded plaintive. She paused but knew she had something she needed to say, "Fred, I have to tell you something. I got a parking ticket today."

"So what?" he said lightly. "Parking badly may be stupid, but it's not going to put you in physical danger, is it?"

"No."

"Then let's get back to the matter at hand." He was stern.

"Fred, I… "

"Not one word, unless you want to go for three nights."

She kept her mouth firmly shut.

"And you will get the cane both nights, two dozen cuts," he added.

Her mouth shot open but he silenced her with a stern glance.

"Over my knees," he said without emotion.

Once she was in position, he began to spank her without mercy, without warm-up, fast and hard. Each slap of his hand causing a loud CLAP as it landed. Each slap caused her to moan and gasp.

It was a long spanking, a very long spanking. There was no mercy, no easy spanks, no slowing down. Finally he finished.

"Lay face down on the bed," he commanded.

She put herself in position. He paddled her; again it was very hard and very fast. The paddle made a sharp CRACK, and her gasps became sharp little yelps of pain. She sounded strangely like a puppy that was accidentally stepped on. Finally, after an unbearable amount of time he stopped.

Just long enough to pick up the leather. WHAP! Although she was used to spankings, she had very seldom been punished, really punished. The forty or fifty with the strap were almost unbearable.

Finally, he gave the order for her to put the paddle away and bring the cane. She did, and then he ordered her to bend over the back of a chair and grab the seat. Normally she got half as many with the cane as with any other implement, but he sternly announced two dozen, and ordered her to ask for them, thank him for each one and keep count.

"Please give me the first," she said softly.

Slash!

"Ah! One, thank you. May I have another?" she managed.

Slash!

"Two, Ouch! Thank you. May I have another?" Her voice was even softer.

"Speak up clearly," he ordered her, "or the stroke won't count."

And so it went, it was the most severe punishment she'd ever received and there was no hint of enjoyment or arousal behind the pain. It was just pain. Pure pain. The full two dozen with the cane almost killed her. At least it felt that way to her.

"Stand in the corner!" he ordered sharply.

Two corner times, two! She thought. I'll kill him. What she did not see, with her nose in the corner, was how badly his hands were shaking, and how pale his face was. It was a long time before he composed himself and told her she could come back to bed.

For the first time after any spanking, fun or discipline, there was no comforting hugs, no aftercare and no lotion tenderly rubbed on the injured area. Also for the first time, there was no cuddling, no tender lovemaking after the spanking.

As she drifted off to sleep she had one question for him. "Fred, why did you wait until after we made love to punish me?"

"I wanted to get rid of any pheromones before you got the spanking," he said coldly. "I wanted to make sure you felt no trace of pleasure from your punishment."

"It worked," she said, still sounding weepy, "believe me it worked."

"And I knew you'd be very sore, and badly marked after," he

added.

"When have soreness and marks ever stopped me from making love?" she sighed, and before morning, they did in fact make love again. Still, she dreaded the night to come. The anticipation was almost worse than the punishment.

The next day she stayed home from work. Not only was she sore, but also she dreaded the coming night.

She woke up feeling queasy and unsettled. The feeling passed but it jogged something in her memory.

That night as a grim Fred came it the door, she had a surprise for him. She had cooked a fantastic dinner for him.

"Time to go upstairs," he sounded resigned.

"I think you might want to change your plans for tonight," she grinned at him impishly.

"Have you come up with a flimsy excuse to get out of your punishment?" he sounded skeptical.

"A way out, yes," she smiled at him. "Flimsy? No. I just found another reason to be extra careful."

She held out the little stick that said, "PREGNANT."

Sometimes you know you are wrong and careless. Sometimes a lesson works to change your ways. Sometimes you just have to grow up and find a new reason to protect yourself and your family.

Three

Couples And Their Toys

How can you get your girlfriend to experiment a little more? Sometimes bringing in another woman is the best way. I know a lot of men and women who switch, so this story is my acknowledgement to them. I'm a natural bottom, but I can get references that when I top, I hit hard. Maybe too hard! I just think that if you're going to do something, you might as well do it right! Put your best effort into it, so to speak.

Marti and Russ hadn't been together long but they were very close lovers. From the moment they met, they each knew this was something special, something rare. Russ had introduced Marti to a new form of play: spankings. Most of the time he was a playful, tender and passionate lover but once in a while he liked to take Marti over his knees for a playful, passionate, sometimes slightly painful spanking. Marti had learned to enjoy it, and the spankings had gradually gotten just a little bit harder, and quite a bit more frequent.

They had only done hand spanking so far; they hadn't tried any toys yet. Russ wanted to, but Marti was resistant. She didn't know why she hesitated but the idea of a paddle or a leather strap gave her the shivers. Playing with toys wasn't the only thing she was resistant to. Russ was also a switch, and he wanted Marti to spank him occasionally but she felt funny and awkward even thinking about it.

So far she had resisted the idea, but she was gradually getting ready to give it a try. Heck, she thought, sometimes spanking Russ seems like a real good idea. He's a good man, but still he's well, a man.

The other thing Marti had resisted was going with him to a place called *The Paddle Club.* Russ had never been himself, so he wasn't able to give Marti any idea of what to expect, and she was afraid the members would be too weird, too kinky for her. And what if going there involved group sex? Yuck!

One day, Russ teased her at work with a series of threatening, teasing and sexy phone calls. The first time he called he was singing and paraphrasing, *Tea for Two,* just the phrase, "Picture you across my knees." Click.

Later it was, "My hand is itching to make sharp contact with your bare bottom." Click.

"Be sure you take your underwear off before you get home, or else." Click.

Another singsong message: "Red and hot, red and hot, that's the kind of bottom you've got." Click.

"Maybe a paddle." Click.

Although they had never used toys, she had heard about them.

"Hey babe," his voice was friendly, low and sexy, "stop at the feed store on 6th and buy me a new riding crop, okay?"

"You expect me to buy you a whip for you to beat me with?" she shrieked.

"A crop, and what makes you think I want to use it on you? Paranoid, much?" Click.

She sat at her desk thinking, fantasizing about the evening ahead. She pictured Russ, his slender build, his black hair, slightly tinged with gray, and his wonderful smile. She ran her fingers through her strawberry blond hair as she daydreamed. Russ loved her hair, loved to tease the bouncy curls, both on her head and the ones lower.

She did as she was told, sort of; she bought the riding crop, but in an act of defiance, she left her underwear on. She drove home wet, excited and nervous. She knew that by buying the crop, she was finally consenting to the use of toys. At least she was consenting to trying toys.

He greeted her at the door with a warm hug and a hot kiss. He took the riding crop and looked it over, swishing it sharply through the air and smiling softly at the uncertainty on her face. He circled a finger lazily in the air.

"Turn around and lift your skirt," he said softly, his brown eyes warm with amusement and a hint of the devil.

Suddenly she was aware of her mistake in defying him about the underwear; she tried to distract him. "Whose car is that in front of the house?"

"I'll tell you," he said carefully, "after. Turn. Skirt up. Now."

She turned, raised her skirt up to her waist revealing that she was still wearing her underwear.

"Oh no," he laughed, "defiant minx."

He swatted her six times with his palm, smart stinging swats. Then he pulled down her underwear and repeated it just a bit harder. He never touched her with the crop.

"Now, pull up your panties, dear." He kissed her cheek. "We have guests."

He led her into the living room.

Marti was torn. Several emotions ran through her. First, she was embarrassed. Had her guests heard her getting swatted? They had to have heard. Second, vaguely disappointed. After all that build-up, that was all they were going to play? What about the crop? And last, panic. Did he mean to introduce her to more than toys? Was this going to be a group sex thing? Why were there strangers in her living room?

She was shaky as she was introduced to Suzanne and James. Suzanne was a woman who just naturally looked regal and elegant. From first appearances, no one ever guessed how down to earth she really was. James radiated warmth, and friendly humor. He was also obviously very deeply in love with Suzanne. Uncertain of what Russ had in mind, she suddenly felt shy in front of the two strangers. She didn't want to meet their eyes, and couldn't think of a word to say. In a flash of panic, she made some weak excuses and quickly left the room. She went to the kitchen, using refreshments for the guests as an excuse for her escape.

"You didn't prepare her very well, Russ," Suzanne looked at

him with accusation in her eyes. "Stay here and talk to James. I'll go talk to her."

She found Marti in the kitchen pouring iced tea. "Can I help?" She wasn't surprised to see tears welling up in Marti's hazel eyes. "You poor thing. I can tell he didn't tell you we were coming or let you decide if you were ready for some group play, did he?"

Marti nodded, obviously miserable. "Does group play include group sex? Because… "

"Oh no!" With a soft laugh, Suzanne jumped in to reassure her, "Not at all. Is that what you thought? No wonder you are so upset! Can I explain?"

At Marti's silent nod, Suzanne continued, "Well, let me tell you what Russ had in mind, and let me reassure you that your part is completely voluntary. Any time we play it has to be consensual and willing, or we do not play. Okay?"

Suzanne sat down at one of the counter chairs. "First of all, James and I are very monogamous. Spanking and being spanked by others is okay but except for a kiss, usually on the cheek as a friendly greeting, no kissing, oral, anal or vaginal sex of any kind is allowed with other partners. Okay?"

Marti nodded wordlessly, relieved. Suzanne continued, "Russ said you liked to play spanking games. He said you liked spanking for fun, but you had never played with toys. He thought you were reluctant and a bit scared of playing with toys. He was interested in learning more about playing with paddles, straps and other toys. He was also interested in learning more about our group."

She paused, "You know James and I are both part of a group called *The Paddle Club*? Well, we have a lot of fun with the group and they're super nice people. We also play with toys a lot. And we know about things like warm ups and after care. Russ thought you might like to well, benefit from our experience. What Russ didn't say is that he was surprising you with us." She paused again. "If you want to play we can, or we can just talk."

"I'd be nervous in a group of strangers," Marti said, and added softly, "and… well, I'm too fat."

"You are not fat," Suzanne said firmly. "We have some members who are fat and you are not even close to it. Pleasingly plump maybe, but not fat."

"Thank you but... "

"No but about it. Those TV stars, models and the rest of them are dead wrong. You are fine." Suzanne told her, "Also we have members from very thin to much heavier than you are, and no one judges them by size. Don't get me wrong, some people prefer to play with a certain type, but they are friendly and respectful to everyone. Also you, my dear, would be very popular *because* of your curves, not in spite of them, and for your personality. Most of our men like a woman with a booty."

At Marti's laugh, Suzanne continued, "Of course, if we do play, you don't have to go bare bottom unless you want to. You can play over your panties, or keep your skirt up. Voluntary means just that," Suzanne grinned at Marti. "About the dirty trick Russ pulled on you tonight, I think you should take the crop to his backside for it, and I mean hard. Don't you?"

Marti was shocked. "What? Crop him? How?"

"Well, he sits on *something* doesn't he? Just get that part of him naked and apply the crop to it."

"To Russ!" Marti squeaked.

"To Russ!" Suzanne nodded. "I know I'd like to. And I will, after dinner." She picked up two of the glasses of iced tea. "Did he at least tell you he had pizza coming?"

When she shook her head, Suzanne laughed and said, "Men!" in such an exasperated tone that Marti laughed too.

"Ready?" Suzanne looked back over her shoulder at Marti.

Marti nodded; it was hard not to feel better after talking to Suzanne who is such an open and friendly woman.

"Russ?" Suzanne said sweetly, "You are going to get it first. Right after the food comes. You deserve it. You didn't explain things to her well enough and let her get upset and confused."

At almost that exact moment the doorbell rang and the pizza was delivered. The four sat and ate their pizza, chatting and relaxing. Marti was surprised at how much she liked these people.

She already saw Suzanne as a friend. James was jovial, polite and like Suzanne, he seemed open and warm.

After the pizza was gone, the paper plates tossed and more ice tea poured, Suzanne turned to Russ. "As I said Russ, you first. Drop 'em and bend over! Marti, find that riding crop Russ told you to buy and use it!"

Russ was surprised but not shocked. He lowered his pants and bent over, his hands on the seat of a straight back chair. Marti used the crop on his bottom timidly, over his jockeys, but she did use it.

Suzanne walked over and pulled the jockeys down. "Now, go for it. A lot harder." Marti tried but she was still timid and filled with hesitation. She handed the crop to Suzanne.

"Now you're gonna get it," she said to Russ. "I won't be as easy on you as she was." Suzanne took over and made Russ's behind red but she never made him squirm or make a sound.

James took care of that however; he took the next turn with the crop and made Russ squirm and gasp, quite easily.

He didn't usually play with men but Suzanne had whispered to him that he should, just to help Marti relax.

Then James himself got the crop used on him. Again Marti did the honors first. She was a little harder with James. Then Suzanne tormented him because she knew his spots and secrets. Russ was just plain severe.

Suzanne was next. First she got an over the knee spanking from both men and then she had Marti use a paddle on her. She coached and nagged Marti until she used the paddle quite hard. Then she knelt over a footstool while Russ caned her. James sat in front of her, kissing her and talking to her in loving tones.

Then it was Marti's turn. James spanked her just a bit harder and faster than Russ ever had, over his knees with his hand. When Marti yelped, he stopped instantly.

"Stop or Go?" he asked.

She never knew why she said, "Go!"

He stepped up the pace just a bit until she said, "Stop!"

After a short break Suzanne introduced Marti to both sides of a hairbrush. Next, Russ used a heavy paddle. James put on a masterful demonstration with Suzanne as his victim, showing his proficiency with a crop, brush, paddle, tawse, cane and rod. He pushed Suzanne to her considerable limits.

"Now Marti, just a taste." James pulled her over his knees for a few from the tawse then had her bend over the desk beside Suzanne for a few sharp cuts of the cane and a few of the rod. He would give her a cut, and then Suzanne next to her a harder whistling cut. Again and again he alternated, letting Marti feel the force of the blows Suzanne received without feeling the sharp, stinging pain.

Everything he did was for her pleasure so that she'd learn to love the sensations and be willing to go a little farther the next time.

Before they finished, James had shown Russ how to use a few other implements on Marti. Implements she loved. He played with ice, fur gloves and feathers, and Suzanne gently ran her acrylic nails over Marti's tender bottom. Each sensation was different, and each one was used between spanks so that her bottom was very sensitive. Finally Russ rubbed lotion over her bottom, stroking and petting for a long, long time.

The two couples sat and talked some more. This time when they mentioned the club, Marti agreed to give it a try.

James and Suzanne invited Russ and Marti over to their house the following week. James offered to show Russ and Marti some rope tricks.

James' parting remark to Marti was, "Next week I'll take you over my knee and spank you, then strip you naked and tie you up before I cane you." When Marti gasped in surprise, he continued, "And you can do the same to me."

"We'll show you how to play safely, even if you're all tied up." Suzanne smiled at Marti's surprise.

Russ and Marti made love long into the night. Just before she went to sleep she said, "Tied up?"

I had already learned a lot by experimentation before I met any spanking friends. Now I know several couples like Suzanne and James. Open, friendly and the best people on Earth, bar none. And I'll refuse to spank anyone who disagrees.

Four

Gee, Thanks Boss

What do you do with an employee who you really like if she just can't seem to do a good job? Do you find someone who can teach her discipline? Do you enjoy the thought of her over a man's knees? Would you want to watch? Or would it only bring back painful memories?

"Rick," Cheryl asked softly, looking down as she always did when she was in his special room. "Can I speak to you for a minute?"

"You know what happens when you try to stall or talk me out of the punishment you so richly deserve," he said softly. It was a warning. "Do you really want to do that?"

"No!" Cheryl looked up, a trace of fear in her hazel eyes. "I meant after, I guess, I just have something I want to discuss with you. Really."

"All right, we'll talk after your punishment." Rick paused, then said firmly, "You do know why you're here today, don't you?"

She had really gotten herself into trouble this time. She'd been good for so long now, that she got complacent. It wasn't just that she'd gone shopping and spent a lot of money. Cheryl's husband Gary wasn't one to worry too much about details like that, as long as all the bills got paid on time without having to dip into their savings.

That was the problem. She'd forgotten to pay the electric bill, the car note and the car insurance. When she looked at the balance on the checking statement and saw that there was quite a bit of money available, she did what any woman would do. She did the "back to school" shopping for the kids, bought some new winter clothes for herself, and even splurged on a sexy dress for an upcoming party she and Gary were going to.

Everything was fine until the electricity was cut off, the credit company threatened to repo the car and the auto insurance expired. Gary went ballistic. He called Rick and set up the appointment immediately to teach Cheryl a lesson. That's why she was squeezed into a morning appointment, and faced working the rest of the day with a very sore bottom. She felt lucky indeed that it wasn't going to be more severe. What if her kids were in the car and she had an accident with no insurance?

"I asked you a question, young lady!" Rick's sharp voice cut into her reverie.

His voice, and looks for that matter, were at odds with his personality. He had shaggy blond hair, almost platinum, and deep blues eyes. He was fit and trim with plenty of muscles. He looked like the prototype of a California beach boy. He should be surfing somewhere instead of... Cheryl cut the thought off to answer him.

"Yes Rick, I know why I'm here." Cheryl hung her head. "I forgot to pay some really important bills this month, which caused all sorts of problems."

"Such as?" he asked quietly.

"It damaged our credit rating when I was late paying the bills, I endangered our family by driving without auto insurance, and even embarrassed my husband. Then I spent the money shopping so we had to cut into our savings account to pay the bills."

"You really did it this time, didn't you?" Rick said softly, "You will stand in the corner for 20 minutes. Use that time to think about what you did. You are going to get a very severe punishment today; in fact, I have your husband's permission to go to any length I feel is necessary. Even the cane."

"The cane!" Cheryl paled, "Rick, believe me, the cane will not be necessary, not if I can help it."

"I'll be back soon." Rick smiled cheerfully as he left the room.

"Don't hurry on my account," Cheryl whispered sadly to his

retreating back.

She knew from painful experience what failure to follow his orders would mean. Without hesitation she stood, reached up under her skirt to lower her panties, pulled up her skirt and stood with her nose in the corner. She hated the waiting but she also knew that when the waiting was over, she'd wish it had taken longer.

Finally, Rick returned.

"Cheryl, come here and we'll begin to teach you a serious lesson about bill paying." He patted his lap.

She placed herself over his knees, felt him raise her skirt and tensed. It was the wrong thing to do because it only made the first hard spank hurt even more. She didn't have any time to worry about it though; that first spank was followed in rapid succession by countless others. The hard spanking covered her whole bottom and the tops of her thighs. It was very long, very hard and very fast. She was pleading and sobbing before it was even half over.

"Shut up!" he commanded sternly.

She tried to follow orders, with only partial success. Finally he stopped spanking her and gently rubbed her shoulders, before telling her in a soft commanding tone to go get the heavy paddle.

"The one with holes, Cheryl," he said firmly but in a surprisingly pleasant voice.

Cheryl turned and actually stamped her foot. "Not the damned drilled paddle!"

Rick's eyes narrowed. He said quietly, "Excuse me? What did you say young lady?"

Cheryl paled, "I'm sorry, Rick."

Realizing she'd made a major mistake, she hurried to get the hated paddle and handed it to him, eyes downcast, but with no further comment. She placed herself into position over his knees without his even asking.

"You do know that little outburst will cost you, don't you?" he asked.

"Does… does it mean the cane?" Cheryl asked, tearfully.

"Not yet. It probably should but I'll give you one more chance," he told her. "Any further disobedience will indeed mean the cane. For this first disobedience, I'll go easy on you and just use the tawse instead of the leather strap."

"Then you know it will go to the cane; I've never made it through the tawse without an outburst!" Cheryl protested.

"You'll just have to try extra hard today," he said coldly. "It's all up to you."

Without any further words he brought the paddle down in a crashing swat. SMACK! And so it began. Cheryl sobbed and pleaded and begged but the rain of merciless blows continued on her bottom and thighs until she was red and splotchy all over. He stopped paddling her and told her to stand in the corner for a short time.

He sat at his desk and sipped a glass of water. He hated punishing sweet Cheryl so hard but he also agreed with her husband: She had forgotten how much she hated the punishment, forgotten all her hard lessons on responsibility and really messed up. She was long overdue for a session and both Rick and her husband agreed that she needed it to be memorable.

He stood up abruptly and fetched the tawse from the cabinet. "Bend over the desk, Cheryl, and let's get this unpleasantness over with. I'll be quick; surely you can take two dozen without any outburst?"

Cheryl paled, "Two dozen?"

"Just hold onto the desk and take it," he said. "It'll be over in less than a minute"

She did try, really, but at the tenth slash of the tawse she was screaming, by the twelfth she was squirming, and there was sweat on her upper lip from her determination to hold on. Of course, neither Rick nor Cheryl realized she was sweating from the strain; they both thought the moisture was only from her tears. By the sixteenth, she thought she was going to die from the effort to hold her place, and by the seventeenth, she broke.

"Dammit! I can't take any more!" She fell to the carpet

sobbing, "I'm sorry, Rick, I just can't!"

"You were so close, too," he said softly. "But you know, I can't let you off." He walked over to the cabinet and put something in his pocket.

"I know," she continued to sob.

He dropped down to the carpet, the tawse in his hand. "You know you need this."

"Yes, Rick," she hiccupped.

Almost gently, he pulled her over his knees and quickly gave her the final seven with the tawse. The strokes were sharp, fast and not really hard. Cheryl realized that even through the pain she was already feeling.

"And now, before the cane you will get ten with the brush for that disobedience."

She squirmed, protesting, "Rick!"

"How many dozen do you want from the cane?"

She shut her mouth and took the ten, once again, though painful they were not the worst she'd ever felt.

"Now, assume the position for a good hard caning," Rick commanded. "I think a dozen will be enough if you take them well."

It took all her courage and determination but she took them well enough so that she only got an extra six. It was over!

"Take all the time you need," Rick said gently. "When you're ready, I'll meet you in the consult room for our talk."

"Thanks Rick." Cheryl smiled through her tears.

"No problem." He grinned as he left the room. "My pleasure."

"Certainly not mine," she muttered.

A short time later she met with Rick in the consult room.

"Have a seat," he offered, handing her a video of her punishment.

She wrinkled her nose at him. "Thanks but I'll stand," she grinned. "Gary's gonna love this tape!" At his quizzical glance she added, "He replays them all the time and the last ones are so old."

"I know," Rick said slowly, "Gary told me he was thinking of having me give you tune up spankings every month if you don't do anything bad enough to get a real punishment."

"I'd get spanked for not being bad?" she asked. "It doesn't seem fair."

"Not a hard spanking, just hard enough to remind you of how badly you hate a real punishment, but that's between you and Gary." He paused, "I don't want to rush you, Cheryl, but… "

"I know, you have to leave soon," Cheryl said softly. "Rick I have a problem with my new secretary, Kathy. I thought maybe you had a suggestion on how I can discipline her."

"What's the problem?" he asked.

"Well, she's a new hire on her 90-day probation, so I could fire her but, dammit, I like the girl," Cheryl sighed. "She's late several days a week and usually misses at least one day completely. Her work is sloppy and poorly done. She's slow and the only filing she does is on her nails! I wish I could send her to you."

"Sounds like she could use the discipline," he agreed.

"On top of that, she wants a raise!" Cheryl's voice rose in indignation.

"Tell me again. Why don't you fire her?" he asked.

"Because I like her as a person and she reminds me of myself before I started coming to you," Cheryl replied slowly.

"I can't take a client without her husband's agreement." Rick only spanked women, and always at their husband's request.

"I know."

"So," Rick grinned, "get his agreement."

"How?" she asked.

"Here's what I'd do." Rick quickly outlined a plan.

"Thanks Rick." She smiled at him. "Good-bye."

"Have a nice day," he said cheerfully. "See you soon."

"Not if I can help it," she threw back at him, laughing.

Back at the office, Cheryl went into the ladies room. She took a few moments for herself to freshen up and had fixed her hair into a soft bun at the nape of her neck. She had pretty hair; the color was deep and rich chocolate, with just a few light touches of gray. At home she usually wore it loose and down, but preferred to pin it up at the office.

"Kathy, before you go to lunch I'd like to see you in my office, please," Cheryl said calmly once she was back at her desk.

"But I was just about to… " Kathy started

"Leave for lunch early?" Cheryl said with a tight smile. "Not today you're not. In my office. Now."

Kathy pouted her way into Cheryl's office and slumped into a chair facing Cheryl's desk. "What is it?"

Cheryl studied the girl for a few moments before replying. Kathy seemed younger, more immature than her twenty years. She was slender with dark brown hair, matched with deep brown eyes. Her face was pretty, heart-shaped and she had great check bones. Cheryl thought to herself that Kathy had probably relied on her pretty looks to get by, and it was time that ended once and for all.

"I want to talk to you about your work and your work habits," Cheryl told her. "You've been with us for about a month and a half, and I'd like to see if you can make some improvements before your 90-day review comes up."

"So that I can get a raise?" Kathy's face lit up.

"So that you can keep your job." Cheryl watched the girl's face drop. "I like you Kathy and I'd like to keep you as my secretary, but your work and your work habits are not up to par. I can go two ways. Either I fire you right now or I try to teach you how to do a good job. I'd like to keep you but some changes need to be made. So I wrote out a review, unofficially, but just like I'd write if your review was due today. I've graded you on several areas." She held out a copy of the paper. "Attendance-zero: 5 missed days in six weeks; Punctuality-zero: 14 incidents of tardiness, 6 late for work, and 8 late returning from lunch. Now I didn't list it here but I notice you often leave early for lunch as well as at the end of the day. Ability to follow direction-3: you are sloppy at following directions, and I expect no less than a 4; Ability to work without direction-0: again, I expect no less than a 4; Attitude-0: Kathy, you just aren't trying!" Cheryl tried to ignore the tears forming in the girl's eyes.

"I do try!" Kathy said protesting. "But there's so much I don't know. It's my first job!"

"And the tardiness?" Cheryl prompted.

"There's a lot of traffic in the mornings!" Kathy wailed.

"And you can't leave home earlier because… " Cheryl said softly.

"I guess I could but I'd have to get up so early!" Kathy said in a tight voice. "We had planned to look for an apartment closer to the city when I got my raise, but now… "

"You have 45 more days; can you get up early that long?" Cheryl asked.

"I can try," Kathy promised.

"Try hard," Cheryl ordered softly.

"How about leaving early for lunch and at the end of the day?" Cheryl asked.

"The lunchroom gets so busy that I try to get there a little early," Kathy said.

"Then change your lunch hour. Try taking it at 11:30 instead of noon. But remember that means you have to be back at work at 12:30 instead of 1:00."

"Okay," Kathy nodded.

"And leaving early?" Cheryl asked.

"To avoid traffic," Kathy said. "The freeway gets tied up real fast."

"Now that's a problem. If you were punctual I'd let you change your hours to 7:30-4:30 to avoid the worst of it, but as it is you'll have to tough it out," Cheryl said.

"All right," Kathy said weakly.

"But the rest of this, the work habits and the attitude, added to your problems with punctuality and tardiness… " Cheryl shook her head. "Kathy, may I speak freely?"

"Yes, of course," Kathy said, sounding puzzled.

"You need discipline," Cheryl said firmly.

"Well I know I need to learn self-dis... " Kathy started.

"No Kathy, you need real discipline," Cheryl said. "Have you had any trouble with you husband about your work habits? Spending habits? Housework?"

"Yes, he's so picky. He treats me like I'm a maid or something," Kathy pouted.

"Well Kathy the bottom line is that for me to keep you on, I want to meet with you and your husband together and discuss this with both of you." Cheryl smiled and a chill went down Kathy's spine. "We'll see if I can come up with a way to help you stay in line. Can he come here at 5 PM?"

"I think he can, let me check. What do you want to see him about?" Kathy asked.

"I'll talk to the two of you together," Cheryl said. "Now go to lunch and think things over."

That evening Kathy's husband, Tom, came in. Cheryl liked him immediately. He was concerned but also friendly. He was good-looking too, with shockingly black straight hair. He looked as if he had Native American blood, but he had bright blue eyes.

They all sat in the office and Cheryl told him much the same things she had already discussed with Kathy. She also asked him about how Kathy was at home.

"I love Kathy but she is really bad with her spending habits; I can't get her to save a penny, and I'd like to own a house someday. The apartment is always dirty from her leaving things all over, and good heavens it's hard to get her to cook. We split the chores up but my list is always done and hers is barely started!"

"You have the easy list!" Kathy protested.

"I'll trade you and see if you think so," Tom offered the challenge. "I'll bet it's the same story, my list done and yours still hanging."

"I have a suggestion," Cheryl added in softly before a real fight started right in her office. "Have you ever given her a good hard spanking?"

"You don't mean… " Kathy's voice rose shrilly.

"Yes, I do," Cheryl was implacable, "if you want to keep your job."

"But I can't spank Kathy!" Tom protested. "It's just not in my nature. It's not something I could do."

"Then I know someone who will do it for you," Cheryl said. "He works out of his house right here in town and specializes in behavior modification. I already made an appointment for you to go talk to him. I suggest the two of you hurry over there for a consult. Now. If you want this job, go there and talk to him. Rick has agreed to stay late to speak to you. And if you sign a contract with him, I will pay for your session and let you leave work for an appointment any time it's necessary."

"Now?" Kathy looked like she was going to cry.

"A consult only, Kathy," Cheryl said. "It won't hurt a bit."

"Honey, she issued an ultimatum to keep your job, so let's go," Tom said gently. He looked up at Cheryl. "We don't have to sign up, do we?"

"No, but go talk to Rick and think it over," Cheryl said. "And Kathy, improve your job performance."

"Honey, this may turn out to be a good thing for us," Tom said quietly once they were in the car.

"Have I been so bad?" Kathy said.

"I love you but yes, you do need to learn some self-control," Tom admitted. "I've often thought that you need a good old-fashioned spanking but I just can't bring myself to do it."

"I'm sorry Tom," Kathy said, "but I still don't think that beating me will solve our problems."

"Spanking."

"Either," Kathy said firmly. "If my parents didn't spank me, why should you?"

"*Because* they didn't spank you, and it's part of your training they missed," Tom said firmly.

"Training for what? To be your slave?" Kathy lashed out.

"Training to be an adult, my partner and my wife," Tom said quietly as he parked in front of Rick's building. "At least listen and think about it, please?"

"I will." Kathy sounded subdued.

"Hi Tom, Kathy, I'm Rick." He held out his hand and gave them both a friendly smile. "Come on in. Please sit down."

"Hi Rick," Tom said, sitting.

"Hi," Kathy muttered, standing near the door, looking as if she was ready to bolt.

It was a look Rick was all too familiar with. "Relax Kathy, we're here to talk. I promise. What seems to be the problem?"

"Kathy is having trouble at work and not doing her chores at home," Tom said. "And she spends far too much money."

"Are you the secretary Cheryl told me about?" Rick asked.

"How do you know Cheryl?" Kathy asked suddenly suspicious.

"She's an old friend," Rick answered discretely.

He went on to describe the program, the advice he gave both husbands and wives, the levels of discipline and how a session went from the time a client entered the room until she left. How a husband and wife together worked out a set of rules for her to follow and how he could call Rick and request him to punish his wife.

"And in your case, Kathy, I would suggest you also give Cheryl the right to set an appointment for you."

He looked straight at Kathy, who had gone pale as a ghost, and told her what missing a punishment session would cost her. He showed them his special room and opened the beautiful wardrobe to show her the paddles, straps, hairbrush and cane. He told them to think it over, discuss it, and gave them a videotape to watch at home.

"This tape is given out with the full permission of the woman in the tape and her husband; it's a fairly harsh level punishment," Rick smiled warmly. "Kathy, please don't let it scare you. She had been really bad, knew it, and asked for it to be very hard. The one thing to understand Kathy is that I do not chase a woman down to beat her. You have to be in full agreement, to sign the contract and stay in the program. Tom can't just sign you up, you have to agree. Do you understand?"

"But who would agree to something like this? Kathy was puzzled.

"Someone who knew, deep inside, that she needed the discipline to learn how to control herself, to be worthy of her husband's love, and to do well in all areas, even her job. Is that you, Kathy?"

She hung her head, and the word barely made it out. "Yes."

"Both of you think it over, talk it over and then when you're both ready come in and sign the contracts," Rick said. "No pressure and no snap decisions."

"Goodnight," he said as they left.

In the car they talked some more. "Tom, do you want me to do this?" she asked.

"Hell no. But I think you need to do it for yourself," he answered her honestly.

"All right," Kathy whispered. "We can sign the contracts tomorrow, but I'm not looking forward to it."

"Honey, I don't think you're supposed to. I think the idea is to try to avoid it by being good," Tom said gently.

"I'll try." Kathy sounded earnest.

Kathy did try, but it was barely a week later that she wound up in Rick's special room waiting for him. Because it was her first time it was a fairly short wait. In just a few moments Rick came in. He talked with her about how she'd been late to work another time. He also told her that Tom was unhappy with the latest credit card bill. Then he told her she would have a bit more corner time, waiting for him to begin.

"I only planned to use my hand and a paddle, but your husband authorized me to also use the strap and the hairbrush if you misbehave," he finished.

She shivered but sat silently.

"Now, when I leave the room you lower your panties to your knees, raise your skirt, and put your nose against the wall right there. Then you just stand there with your nose in place quietly until I return. When I come back we can get this over with."

"Yes, Rick," Kathy's voice trembled. "I'm so scared because

it's my first time."

"Kathy, honey," Rick said firmly but gently.

Kathy looked up at him. "Yes?"

"You'll be more scared next time, I promise." Rick left the room.

Before long Rick returned. He pulled the straight-backed chair out into the center of the room and sat in it.

"Come here Kathy," he ordered. She moved over closer to him but kept herself out of easy range. "Closer."

She moved slowly closer. He caught her hand and pulled her firmly over his knees. Her panties were still down around her knees and he pulled her skirt out of his way.

Without another word the spanking began. There was no warm up and no let up. It was a long hard spanking and it had barely started when Kathy began to cry and squeal. She struggled to get off Rick's lap. The spanking continued, moving down to the backs of her legs and up again to her bottom which was already turning hot and red. Finally she let out with a string of curses that would make a sailor blush.

"That kind of language will earn you an extra implement," Rick said firmly. "Do you want a dozen with the strap added on?"

"No sir," Kathy said crying, "I'm sorry."

"And so you should be." He spanked her harder still.

It was a struggle but she managed to keep herself from swearing at him for the rest of the spanking. He let her up.

"Now go to the cabinet and get the paddle, the leather one without the holes," he ordered.

Reluctantly, she complied, tears were running freely down her face.

"Hand it to me." He held out his hand and she placed the paddle in it. "Now back over my knees."

She moved slowly, reluctantly, but she did it. Secretly Rick was proud of her but he didn't let it show. He paddled her with very fast hard strokes, each one causing her to squeal and wiggle.

After the fifth one she said, "Ouch! Dammit!"

"That's it, you'll get a dozen with the strap for that," he said softly.

"I'm sorry, Rick," she muttered.

"I know Kathy, but that's not the point, is it? The point is for you to learn how not to get into a situation where you need to be sorry," he told her pointedly. "I had only planned to give you 10 with the paddle but now, I think we'll go for 15." And those next ten were delivered swiftly and with a harshness that left Kathy speechless, fortunately for her.

Again, he let her up. "Put this back in the cabinet and fetch me the leather strap, the one with one solid piece, not the split one. That's a tawse, by the way."

She did as directed, knowing she was in for it. She handed it to him with so much reluctance that even Rick was tempted to smile, but he remained impassive. "Now Kathy, bend over the desk grabbing the other side and hold on. If you move, we start over."

"All over?" her eyes widened.

"From the first stroke of the strap," he said, to clarify the matter. "Now I'm only going to give you six since this is your first time. It's usually at least twelve. This should take less than 30 seconds if you hold on, stay in position and do not swear. You can do that for me can't you, Kathy? You have to remember, I will not show you any mercy. If you earn more strokes or another implement, you will get it. You are the only one who can make this punishment end. Do you understand?"

"I... I'll try," Kathy stammered.

To the amazement of both, she did. Rick told her to stand and stroked her shoulder gently. "You did real well." Impersonally, he handed her a box of tissues. "Put your clothes back on and go in there to wash your face. I will have a tape ready for you to show Cheryl and Tom when you're ready to leave. Now thank me for spanking you."

"Thanks, Rick," she whispered.

"No problem Kathy, see you soon."

"I hope not!"

"All the girls say that," he laughed. "I'm going to get a

complex."

Kathy drove back to her office and sheepishly walked over to Cheryl's office door. She rapped gently and heard Cheryl call for her to come in. "I'm back."

"Are you okay?" Cheryl asked with concern. "Come on in and let's talk a minute. Sit down."

"Yes, I'm fine, but I'd rather stand," Kathy said with a wry grin. "Sit!"

"All right." Kathy sat gingerly.

"What implements?" Cheryl asked.

"Hand, paddle and strap," Kathy replied. Then without thinking she asked, "How do you know?"

"The implements?" Cheryl grinned and explained. "I'm a client. My husband Gary loves to spank me, but only for fun. He thought using spanking for real discipline would take the fun out of it, so we use Rick for the real discipline and still have fun when we play. It works for us. Let me see the tape."

Blushing, she handed the tape to her boss. "Do you want me to leave while you watch it?"

"No." Cheryl was already starting the tape.

When it was over Cheryl told her, "My last appointment with Rick was the day I gave you that early review. It was much harder than what you got."

"Then how could you?" Kathy burst into tears. "You knew how it would be... "

"And I knew how much you needed it. Without Rick's help, I'm so much like you, it's scary," Cheryl told her.

"But it hurt so bad!" Kathy sobbed.

"And your point is?" Cheryl asked softly.

"I don't want to go back there ever," Kathy wailed.

"You can avoid it by following the rules you and Tom drew up," Cheryl said. "There's no trap there. Rick would love not to have to see you again," she paused, "but he will sooner or later, and we both know it. Between here and home, you'll misbehave."

"And how will Tom know it if you don't report me?" Kathy asked.

"That's not even a question because I will report you. For your own good," Cheryl said with a smile.

"Gee thanks," Kathy said bitterly. Then she paused and gathered herself, "No, I mean that. It surprises me to say it but thank you, really."

"You're welcome." Cheryl walked around the desk and hugged the girl. "So, go get back to work. And Kathy, you can file standing up." She winked.

Kathy let herself into the small apartment only to find Tom waiting for her.

"How are you sweetheart?" he asked gently.

"I'm fine, bruised, but fine." She looked up at him, "Do you want to see the tape?"

They sat together and watched the tape. Kathy winced and cringed at several points but the only place that really embarrassed her was when she swore at Rick. Tom was transfixed. He saw the girl he loved being hurt, but knew that she was also being helped. He recognized when Rick had eased up on her, for her first time, and he saw how fairly Rick reacted to her bad language and how patiently he put down her defiance.

"I think we picked the right man for the job," Tom commented. "He was very patient with you, and he took it easy on you when things got too painful."

"That was easy?" Kathy was surprised. "It didn't feel like it!"

"No it was severe and I'm sure it was very painful, but he held back with the last few with the paddle and also with the strap," he told her. "Watch the tape, you can tell that he knows when you've had enough."

"I see what you mean," Kathy said slowly. "Does that mean I can trust him not to take things too far?"

"It means two things: You can trust him not to take things too far, and next time will be harder, much harder."

"I'm not looking forward to it," she admitted.

"It's not like it's scheduled," Tom pointed out. "All you have to do is follow the rules, and you don't have to go back. Ever."

"What are the odds of that?" Kathy laughed.

"I've got next Tuesday in the bet with Cheryl." He smiled at her.

"Tell Cheryl that I've got my money on her going back before I do," she told him archly.

"Good plan." Tom took her hand, "Let's go to bed."

"I'm not sleepy."

"Neither am I."

They made love with a tenderness and a passion that surprised both of them, long into the night. Kathy was almost late for work the next day but she made it on time.

In the end the 'bet' between Cheryl and Kathy was a tie, but that's another story.

Funny, how one woman can know exactly what it would take for another woman to reach her full potential as a woman. Is it greater friendship to make sure she gets it or to shield her from the results of her own actions?

Five

Tender Lovemaking

Mutually agreed upon spankings in the privacy of your (my!) own home. Does it sound boring? Hardly! With the right person it can be exciting and romantic! Of course, with the right person almost anything can be exciting and romantic.

Wendy and Dick had only been dating a very short time. Their relationship was still very new; so new they had not even made love yet. They both wanted to, but Wendy kept saying that she wasn't ready to make love, not yet.

Dick respected that, after all he wanted to date someone with morals and ethics. He was a kind and decent man himself. He was also impatient, but wise enough to keep that to himself. Outwardly he was patient with just enough urgency to add a bit of spice to the relationship.

Wendy told Dick she was really not sure why she was holding back. True, she was raised with a fairly good religious background, but she had fallen out of the habit of going to Church. She had her own version of morals and ethics though, and in that she has not strayed too far from how she was raised. She simply believed, deep inside her heart, that she would know when the time was right.

For his part, Dick was a decent man who respected her feelings. He wanted to make love to her but he avoided resorting to seduction and persuasion, as hard as that was for him. He preferred to let Wendy come to the decision on her own. That didn't stop him from asking, he was human after all.

He accepted her polite refusals with basic dignity, at least outwardly. He secretly savored his realization that those refusals were obviously getting harder for Wendy. Self-denial was costing Wendy more and more as time went on.

He knew instinctively that what was growing between him and Wendy would be special and long lasting. It scared him, just a bit, as he was not ready to find the love of his life. He was not ready for a big commitment. The thought of marriage gave him the cold shakes. But he looked forward to keeping Wendy in his life, and those cold shakes were getting warmer. Thoughts of commitment became less frightening. He finally admitted to himself that he would do anything to keep her in his life.

They had met at a friend's party, and spent most of the evening outside avoiding the crowd in the small living room. They sat on patio chairs, each with a glass of wine, and talked for hours. When Dick asked Wendy for a date the next night, it was the start of a marathon of dating.

In the short time since that party, they had gone out on lots of dates. Dates that usually ended up on her sofa, with the two of them engaged in some rather passionate lip locks.

They had been out to dinner many times, and played foot games under the table while gazing longingly at each other. They had also seen a few movies and missed half the action because they were necking in the dark. They had gone dancing and done some very close, very slow dancing, even when the music was fast. They had gone on a picnic at the beach and spent most of the time rolled up in their beach blanket. Wendy had even fixed Dick a fancy dinner at her apartment, but they let the dinner burn while they made out on the sofa.

There were certainly some flaming hot, wild and passionate necking sessions that stopped just short of sex. Too short. They had not had sex of any kind, even oral. They had not used their hands to bring each other to orgasm. In fact, so far, all their clothing had remained in place.

Dick was willing to wait for the sex because he had a feeling that what was building up between the two of them was going to be something very special, something well worth the wait. There was a streak of another emotion under the suppressed passion, something infinitely more tender and lasting, that made the wait worthwhile.

He was, of course, getting more and more impatient. He was much less willing to wait, and much more ardent than he had been at the start of their passionate, but still unconsummated relationship.

On Wendy's birthday, her twenty-fourth, Dick took her out for a great dinner at a very expensive restaurant. After their meal, they went to a nightclub that featured music from the forties and fifties for some ballroom dancing. He preferred dancing with Wendy to music that allowed him to hold her in his arms. He loved the feel of her slender body close to his trim, hard form. He also liked her in the clothes she wore when they went dancing to the slower music. She always wore something flowing, feminine and soft.

For her birthday, she was wearing a dress with a full skirt; it was made of a soft, shimmering fabric that seemed almost alive as it swirled around her knees. It was a powder blue that meshed perfectly with the blue floral print of the slightly low-cut bodice. The whole effect was to really set off her wide blue eyes. With her long, soft and straight blonde hair she looked like Alice in Wonderland but Alice all grown up, quietly seductive, yet somehow still soft and innocent.

Before dinner he had given her a very beautiful, delicate and expensive gold bracelet that she immediately put on and swore never to take off. When he finally took her home after the dinner and dancing, he wanted to give her one more thing. He wondered how she would react to his final surprise.

He stood facing her just inside her front door. His hands were resting on her shoulder but slowly they began to drift down her back.

"Wendy," he began, sounding almost nervous. His hands had drifted down as far as her firm, round bottom, and rested there gently stroking. "There is something else I want to do for your birthday. It's a sort of birthday tradition."

He planted tender kisses all over her face as one of his hands

63

smacked her bottom almost tenderly.

"Yes, Dick," she said softly, looking into his warm brown eyes and feeling that, at last, the time was right.

Imagine her surprise and shock when he sat down on the sofa and she found herself being pulled over his knees with her full, swirling skirt tossed up over her back. She got the first birthday spanking of her life right on her lacy pink panties! It was the first spanking of any kind in her life! SMACK!

Unfortunately for Wendy, it was not a soft, fake, playful spanking, like most birthday spankings. It was not especially hard, but it was real and it really smarted. The last swat, the *one to grow on*, was even quite a bit harder than all the rest! That one really stung! Even over her panties it made a resounding crack! When Dick was finished, he let her up.

She jumped to her feet and stood before him gasping indignantly, her cheeks bright pink and her blue eyes wide. She couldn't begin to realize how beautiful she looked.

"How could you do that?" she practically shrieked, one hand rubbing her behind.

"Hey! I asked first, and you said I could! What do you mean, how could I?" Dick protested. Completely bewildered, he ran his hand through his wavy brown hair. "It was just a little birthday spanking!"

"I didn't say yes to a spanking. Who would?" she protested sputtering. "We don't do birthday spankings in my family! In fact, no one has ever spanked me."

"Then what did you think I was asking you?" He was completely perplexed. "If you weren't agreeing to a birthday spanking then what was that 'Yes, Dick' all about?"

"The question that you *always* ask me, stupid. I was saying *yes*. I want to go to bed with you!" She was angry. In fact, she was practically shouting at him by now. She paused and took a deep, slow breath before continuing more calmly, "I decided that I'm finally ready for us to make love. How was I to know you had something else on your mind? You sure never did before."

"How could you miss it? It's your birthday, I had my hands all over your bottom, and I even gave you a little smack!" He was getting a bit frustrated and his voice was getting a little louder as he tried to explain and salvage the situation.   "And it's a tradition. How could you have a happy birthday without a birthday spanking?"

"We don't do birthday spankings in my family."

"Oh." His heart seemed to sink down to his feet; this was what he had waited for, his big chance. Had he blown it? He felt scared and very, very dumb. "So you were thinking of that other question. The one I always ask you."

"Yes, dummy, I already said that," she said sounding icy. "What I said yes to was sex, not a spanking."

"The sex question… Well… " He struggled to regain some of the ground that he had lost. "It wasn't like you were being forced to make a choice, either one or the other.   Either you get a birthday spanking or we make wild passionate love all night long. You can still say yes to both." He gazed at her hopefully and said earnestly, "I agree that we are ready for the next step. I more than agree. I've been going crazy waiting for us to make love. I know that it would be more than just sex between us." He pulled her down onto his lap, cuddled her and kissed her neck tenderly. "I want to give you my love and my passion. I already gave you the spanking, I can't take it back. Why couldn't I give you both? The spanking and my love, I mean." He pulled her into his arms for a long, hard kiss.

It only took an instant for Wendy to respond. She poured all her feelings into the kiss. She thrust her tongue deeply into his mouth in a gentle and still frantic duel with his.   Her hands tangled in his hair as she wiggled on his lap. She pulled back, her breasts rising and falling with each breath as she looked deeply into his eyes.

Not trusting herself to speak, she reached out and unzipped the fly on Dick's pants. It seemed to be a definite enough answer for him.   He stood and picked her up and carried her into the bedroom. He placed her gently on the bed.

She lay there and looked shyly up at Dick. "I know that I

65

made you wait a long time for this, I mean, for us to make love. Longer than most people wait these days. There's a reason I wanted to go so slow." She paused, swallowing several times before continuing, "It's because you see, I know it's not uh, fashionable, but I'm a virgin."

Somehow Dick was not surprised, although he knew very few women kept their virginity until they were twenty-four.

"Are you sure you want to make love with me? Are you sure you're really ready? Remember, you still have a choice," Dick asked gently, with concern, in between planting soft kisses all over her face. Suddenly he laughed, "But please, please don't change your mind. Please say yes."

"Yes. I'm sure, very sure. I want you so much." She responded to his kisses and began to work open the buttons on his shirt. "It's strange, I feel like I don't have any choice, but not because you're pressuring me. Just because if I don't make love to you right now, I think I'll die. It's just a good thing we're not still out in public because I'd probably do something that would get us both arrested."

"Thank God! I want you too," he managed between kisses on her throat.

"What?" She was so dazed she wasn't sure she was following the conversation.

"I don't mean I want you to do something in public and get us arrested. I mean I really want you, any time and any place," he managed before putting his mouth to much better use.

He turned her around. Then, trailing kisses along her soft neck, he unzipped her dress. He pushed the soft, silky material down off her shoulders, following the fabric with his mouth.

He unfastened her bra and she slid it off. She turned to face him again, pulling his shirt wide open baring his chest, and began to kiss and suck gently, almost shyly, on his nipples. The dress fell in a soft swirl landing around her feet. She only had her lacy pink panties and silky pantyhose on.

He pulled the bedspread down and turned back the blankets. She pulled off her pantyhose, then he took off her panties. He walked around behind her and kissed her right on the barely pink splotches he'd made on her slender bottom. She blushed, savoring the strange feeling of his mouth on her buttocks, then she sat down on the edge of the bed and watched him. He finished taking off his shirt and pants and came to stand in front of her.

She reached out and slowly lowered his underwear, carefully maneuvering the material over his erect manhood. She looked at his fully erect cock and smiled, moving back on the bed and reaching up for him.

He climbed up onto the bed with her and took her into his arms. Going slowly and using all his patience, he aroused her completely. He used his mouth and hands on every inch of her lovely body. He stroked and suckled her breasts for a long time. He used one hand to gently tease the tangle of curls at the apex of her thighs, and then with that same hand he started slowly and gently stroking her even more intimately, finding the nub that was the very core of her arousal. He watched her face as he built the rhythm and pressure of his strokes up to a fast feverish rhythm that sent her over the edge.

She cried out with the force of her first real orgasm. Then she lay back on the bed looking dazed and shivering slightly. He never stopped playing with her lovely body. He just eased up to gentle kisses and stroking her face and neck. As soon as she drifted back to reality, he started to arouse her to the flash point once more. This time it was even easier for him; she was so responsive that he already knew her most sensitive areas, her strongest pleasure points.

"Dick, I want to pleasure you, too. What can I do?" she asked, moaning softly. "I feel like I'm just taking from you this way."

"Just let me do all the good stuff for now. You are pleasuring me by letting me take care of you." He kissed her tenderly, "This is only the first time, next time you take the lead and explore if you want. You can map out my pleasure spots and find out what I like the most, okay?"

He trailed his mouth down her body, kissing her navel, and

moved lower. He brought his mouth down on her warm, moist pussy and using his tongue and teeth he took her to the peak once more. Again he sent her flying off into space, screaming and shivering with the force of another wild orgasm.

He cuddled and stroked her again, going back to the start, building her pleasure step by step. She was more than ready when he slowly and using great gentleness entered her, stretching her virgin cunt, and tearing her hymen. She felt the pain, but it was insignificant compared to the pleasure.

He paused, letting her get used to the feel of him inside her, and began to move gently at first, then gradually building to a feverish pitch. He slowed down just before they reached their orgasms, prolonging the pleasure. Over and over, he took them almost to the brink and then retreated before he finally took them over the peak into a spinning, shattering crescendo.

Basking in the afterglow, Dick was overwhelmed with his feelings of tenderness for Wendy.

"Did I hurt you, sweetheart?" he asked. "Was it all right?"

"Which part, that hard spanking or the sex?" She gave him a sideways glance, full of mischief.

"That wasn't a hard spanking, just a loving little bottom warmer. I meant the sex, was it good?" He gave her a kiss on her forehead.

"All right?" He gave her a kiss on her chin.

"At least better than doing the dishes?" He gave her a kiss on the breast.

"The sex was great! Fantastic! Worth waiting for!" She punctuated her exclamations with kisses on his chest, each one moving a little lower. "Too good for us to wait very long before we do it again."

"I was surprised that you were a virgin." He paused, watching the progress of her mouth as she worked her way down his body. "Would it be too stupid for me to ask why now? Why me?" He was curious.

"Because I love you and it felt right." She was totally assured and confident in her love. She smiled softly at him, "It's as simple as that."

"Good. That's the best reason because I love you too," he said, using one hand to raise her face so he could look directly into her eyes.

She looked at him for a long moment, then gathering her courage lowered her mouth to his body again, suckling his nipple before moving down to his navel. She moved her mouth down lower still.

He ran his fingers through her hair as she took his large cock into her mouth. It was the first time she had ever done it. She was a bit tentative and awkward but she was also gentle and loving. Her very innocence aroused him even more. He closed his eyes and savored the pure sensations that she made him feel. After a while he pulled her gently up and lifted her astride his body and they began to make hot, sweet love again.

The relationship took on a whole new life from that point on. Soon, Wendy gave up her apartment and moved in with Dick. She had always believed she would not live with a man until she was married, but somehow it seemed right.

Their social life changed too. Friends rarely saw them, and never saw them apart. Dinners got shorter, and now they always skipped dessert. They started going only to restaurants that were close to home. Movies were much less frequent and they usually walked out, hand in hand, somewhere in the middle. Dancing was almost eliminated entirely; they rarely stayed in a nightclub for more than two songs! And, after that memorable night, the only picnic they went on was rudely interrupted by a very unsmiling policeman at a very tender, private and embarrassing moment. But the sex was terrific! Fantastic!

Wendy proved to be a passionate, giving and imaginative lover who could never get enough. She was great to be around out of bed too, with a warm and generous nature and a strong sense of humor.

Not that things were perfect. They had their rough moments. Neither of them was particularly tidy, but they managed to keep the apartment livable. They took turns with most household chores but Wendy usually cooked. They argued over what to watch on TV. Dick preferred going out and playing sports. The only sport he would watch on TV was golf.

Wendy played golf, but never watched it on TV. Instead, Wendy could curl up and watch every football game she could find, and plenty of baseball, hockey and basketball too. She read romances and blood-curdling mysteries. Dick read the Wall Street Journal, although he had also read some of Wendy's mysteries, and even secretly read some of the romances. He was shocked at the love scenes. How intense and explicit they were. This was soft-core porn, or damn close to it.

Dick fell even more in love with Wendy everyday. He showed her every sexual trick he knew, and together they found some new ones. They made love all over the house, from the kitchen sink to the top of the clothes dryer while it was running. It really vibrated, but not as much as the washing machine when it was on the final spin cycle! Now *that* was crazy and wild. Every inch of floor, every chair, sofa and table now held sensuous memories for them.

One night they were talking about just that, their sexual experimentation, when Wendy lazily asked, "So, what haven't we tried?"

Dick looked into her eyes, "I can think of several things, not all of which I want to do."

"Let's hear them so we can discuss it." She was always ready for new ideas.

"First, threesomes or group sex," he said, then put his mouth to her breast.

"Awww, ahhh, ugh! Yuck! Not that! I only want you," she moaned as he suckled.

"Good, I'd hate it. I don't want to share any part of you." He moved on to the other breast, paused then said with a laugh, "I have some friends who told me that they use an inflatable man or woman as an extra sexual partner for role playing, to pretend that they are in a threesome. I personally think that sounds too silly to be real fun."

"Sounds weird to me. We'll talk about it later; it may be crazy, but it could be fun someday. I'd probably laugh myself sick but at least you wouldn't get too jealous." She looked suspiciously at him and asked, "What friend told you this? Huh! And they say all women brag about sex. What's next?"

"Second, sodomy." He moved his mouth down to her abdomen.

"You know me, for you I'll try anything," she moaned. "What else?"

He raised his mouth slightly, "We could try sexual spankings, maybe even some BDSM, although I'm not really into BDSM."

"We did that!" Wendy protested weakly. "The spanking part!"

"No, that was a birthday spanking. Entirely different. But did it hurt or turn you on? Did you like it?" Dick moved his tongue into her navel.

"Actually, I sorta did." She ran her fingers through his hair. "I was just afraid to say so because you might try it again, harder. But how is it entirely different? I mean, you still use your hand to slap my bottom and cause me pain."

"Wendy, lovey, the point of sexual spanking isn't to cause anybody any real pain. It's to make things exciting and a little kinky between two people. It sure wouldn't be exciting if the spanking was too hard for the one getting spanked to enjoy it." Dick's fingers were in the soft hair at the apex of her thighs. "And for the record, it wouldn't always have to be your butt. It could be mine."

"Why don't I really believe that?" she moaned softly. "So do you want to spank me?"

She was still not certain, but she was turned on. She wasn't entirely sure if it was the totally outrageous idea or his busy fingers and warm mouth that aroused her.

"Only if you want it too." His mouth followed his fingers and found a tender target, the moist sweet warmth of her sex.

"I do," she responded, with the last of her coherent words before her moans took over.

Dick raised his mouth. "Remember that phrase my love

because the last thing we haven't tried is marriage."

"Do you want to *marry* me?" she asked, amazed. All she was really trying to do was get what he was saying straight in her startled brain.

"Nice of you to ask, I accept!" In the future, he'd always say that he had tricked her into doing the proposing.

He kissed her and suddenly, even as they kissed, they were both laughing.

Wendy was stunned, it was unbelievable! Marvelous! Fantastic! Too good to be true!

She managed one word, "When?"

"I'm open to anything from a fancy, formal affair even to driving to Las Vegas tonight and finding a tacky wedding chapel," he told her. "As long as it's soon!"

"Las Vegas sounds good to me. Let's go now!" She jumped up out of bed, pulled a dress over her head, no bra, no underwear and no stockings. She got out her overnight bag and only put in her toothbrush, a swimsuit and a robe. "Well, I'm packed, what's holding you up?"

"I thought we could take care of this first." He gestured at his erection, laughing.

"Oh, well, if you absolutely insist," she grinned wickedly. "As long as you're not trying to stall or back out."

She pulled her dress up and straddled him, riding his cock like an expert.

When they were both hot, sweating and gasping she looked at him almost shyly, "Do you mean it? Really?"

"Yes, pack a few more things and call your boss at home. Try to get at least a week off and I'll call my secretary and arrange to be off too." Dick had his own accounting firm. "After we're married we can stay in Vegas, or drive back to my cabin at Big Bear. We can go as soon as we're packed and we've made our calls. But first I'm going to take a long, hot shower."

They eventually got to Las Vegas and found the aforementioned tacky wedding chapel. In a ceremony marked by a scratchy recording of the Wedding March and artificial flowers, with a minister dressed up like Elvis, they became man and wife. The ceremony was flashy and ridiculous. Who cared? It was perfect.

Afterwards they drove back to Dick's cabin at Big Bear Mountain. Dick carried her over the threshold and into the bedroom dropping her on the king-sized bed.

He reached up under her skirt and pulled down her underwear saying, "Well wife, I want you to remember who's going to wear the pants in this family."

Rolling her over, he pulled up her dress and reached into the drawer beside the bed. He took out a jar of lubricating jelly and spread it all over her ass. He gave her a hearty spanking, harder and a lot longer than the birthday spanking had been. Each loud slap landing sharply on her lovely ass, causing her buttocks to jiggle as they turned red and became hot.

"So," he said when he stopped, "what do you say to that?"

He stood beside the bed and grasped her hips, raising her up onto her hands and knees.

"Ouch?" she replied with a laugh.

Using the same jar of lubricating jelly he gently lubricated her anus, working one and then two fingers in and out. As she relaxed, he finally managed to insert a third finger.

"Now it's time to take your last virginity," he said, sliding her to the end of the bed and standing behind her.

He lubricated his large cock, and using a great deal of patience and gentleness slid into her anus. He took it slow and easy until she relaxed and began to moan with arousal, then he began to race to a passionate climax. For a long moment they both seemed poised on the brink before they crashed into a whirlpool of sensation. He climbed onto the bed beside her and held her in his arms, cradling her gently. They began to relax, talking softly about their new lives together as husband and wife.

They got out of bed, finally undressing, and went into the shower where they spent most of the time soaping and arousing each other. When they got out of the shower Dick dried her gently using the rough texture of the terry cloth to arouse her even more; they never even got completely dried off before they returned to the bed.

As soon as she got on the bed she reached for him. "Now use your cock to pound me into the mattress!"

They made hard furious love. There was a new edge to it; they reached a peak they had never reached before. When it was over she was shaking and breathless.

When she recovered enough to speak, she looked up at him, "I thought a honeymoon was time for tender lovemaking."

"Well, we sure made love and I'll bet that your ass is tender, so I guess we got that right." He gave her a long, loving look, "Was it okay? Did I hurt you?"

"The spanking, the sodomy or the sex? You want the truth? I loved them all!" She rolled over onto her side and rubbed her still warm ass. "Can I return the favor sometime? The spanking I mean."

He abruptly got out of the bed. She sat up and watched him, admiring his naked body as he wandered around the tiny cabin. She wondered what he was up to. Finally he went outside, still naked.

When he came in he was carrying a piece of rubber hose about a foot long. He gave it to her, and then lay down on his stomach with his head on his hands. Immediately, without any hesitation, she got up off the bed and gave him a fairly severe whipping, stopping instantly as soon as he said, "Enough!"

He had a hard-on from the whipping; she took one look at it and said, "Let's not waste that!"

"We sure won't, but remember," as he slid into her softness, "we can always get another!"

"Lord, I hope so!" She pulled his head down to her breast, smiling and sighing softly as he began to tease the nipple. "I hope we feel this way when we're ninety."

"I don't want to feel this way when I'm ninety." Dick protested.

"Why not? Everything's great," she looked at him, suddenly uncertain, "isn't it?"

"No, there's something missing," he said seriously. "I need something else, something more out of life than this."

"What more can you possibly want?" she asked, feeling slightly hurt. "Children?"

"Not now, but soon." He kissed her. "That's not what I meant."

"Then what?" She was totally puzzled.

"Food!" Dick laughed. "I'm starving."

Wendy laughed back, "Just like a man. Once you marry one he turns out to be all stomach and no action." After that insult, those were the last words she spoke for a very long time. Of course Dick didn't get his dinner for a very long time either. He didn't care.

Ain't love grand? Ain't spanking great? I was sorting out my feelings last night after tying myself up and waiting for my lover. Did I like it? Today I found myself trying to find a better table to bend over and a softer rope. I must really like it!

Six

My Butt Belongs To Daddy

A father's love can be intense, so can a father's anger. What do you do when she's gone wild? What is your biggest fear? Or maybe I should ask: Who is your biggest fear?

It was a nightmare! Matt couldn't believe the changes he saw in his fifteen-year-old daughter, Sally. It had been a terrible year for both of them, father and daughter. Matt's wife had died in a terrible car accident and to escape his intense grief, he had shut off his emotions. He became cold and unfeeling, and buried himself in his work. As his shock and grief faded, he gradually began to come to terms with his loss. Finally he realized how badly he had failed, and how much his daughter needed him. It was a bitter truth for him to admit, even to himself, that he was neglecting his teenaged daughter.

Eventually, as he began to heal and slowly pull himself up from the depths of his despair, he became aware that his daughter needed him, his help, his love and support. After all, she had suffered a shocking loss too. She had lost her mother! For that matter, Matt ruefully admitted to himself, she might as well have lost her dad. He had spent so much extra time at work that it seemed he was never home. He was ashamed that he had ignored her. She was in a delicate stage of a girl's life and she had suffered a tremendous loss. Matt made a resolution to himself that he would become a better father. He would stop hiding himself in his work and instead overcome his sorrow by helping his daughter cope with hers.

Matt knew the girl had problems, most of which he attributed to her grief. Her grades were slipping. She was lying to him all

76

the time about anything and everything. She had a rebellious attitude. She wore tight clothes and short skirts. She used too much make-up and her long blond hair looked wild and unkempt. Lately she always had a sullen expression twisting her pretty face, with defiance in her brown eyes. He had found cigarettes in her room when he was putting her clothes away. Matt was sure there was a boy involved, and it was probably an older boy.

He decided to spend some extra time at home giving Sally more of his time and more of his love. He arranged to take a week off work on the Friday before Spring Break. Maybe a trip to the cabin would give them a chance to relax and talk; they might begin to bridge the gap between them. He got the surprise of his life that night when he came home from work three hours early. Sally was home and so was her boyfriend.

His worst fears were confirmed in an instant. She was letting her boyfriend seduce her; not just into sex but also into all the worst teenage vices. When he walked into the house he found beer cans in the living room. Cans that had not been there when he left! There was the distinctive smell of marijuana in the air, and worst of all he heard laughter from Sally's bedroom upstairs. Male laughter.

He ran up the stairs and into Sally's room without bothering to knock. He got the shock of his life. His sweet, innocent, baby was in bed with her latest boyfriend. The guy seemed to be several years older than Sally. They both looked up, horrified at the abrupt intrusion.

Sally shrieked, "Daddy!"

Matt found his voice and without looking at the guy he asked, "Who in the hell are you?"

"Paul." The word came out with a trace of bravado.

"Paul, if you have any desire to live to see tomorrow, get out of that bed right now. Get your clothes and go to the living room. Get dressed and wait there for me. If you leave I will press charges against you for statutory rape and drug charges." This was no idle threat; every word had the ring of absolute truth.

Paul couldn't leave the room fast enough.

Matt tried to control his temper; he took a deep breath and strained to get a grasp on his emotions. He looked around the room staring blankly at anything he could find, trying to focus on something neutral. Trying to avoid looking at his teenage daughter in the bed. Naked. His glance fell on the dresser, on a small hand mirror with traces of white powder on it. It took just a moment for the significance of it to sink in. That was the final straw! His rage was matched only by his fear. He had a sick feeling in the pit of his stomach!

He had never believed in corporal punishment but his mind changed immediately. Sally, looking into his face, knew it as soon as he did. Matt pulled himself together and spoke. His voice was surprisingly calm.

"Sally, I know I haven't been much of a father to you since your mother died and I'm very sorry, but that doesn't mean you can do whatever you want. I've had it! I'm very sorry I was so stupid that I let my grief overwhelm me. I know I neglected you. I know you're in pain too. Ever since I noticed the changes in you, I've tried to be patient. I thought I could wait out this rebellious period of yours. I thought it was normal teenage rebellion. Maybe I didn't really think. I know what you've been through, but I can't ignore this!" He paused, "I love you too much." He took a deep breath and continued, "So here it is. You are going to have a choice. Either you accept some severe punishment, painful punishment, or you leave this house right now! If you leave, you won't be allowed to come back until you decide to change your ways. You will agree to live by the rules that I'm going to set down. One more thing; don't expect to move in with Paul if you leave home because if you don't stop seeing him or if you fail to submit to your punishment, I will have him arrested! I will press charges against him for statutory rape, drug use, giving alcohol to a minor, anything that I can find. I will make his life a living hell. How old is he? If he's over eighteen, I may be able to get him put in prison!"

"Daddy!" Sally was crying. "Daddy, I'm sorry. Please don't

throw me out! Daddy. Please, I'm sorry. I'll take any punishment if you will forgive me when it's over."

"I will punish you and I can forgive you, but it's going to take a long time for me to trust you again, if I ever can. Let me think." He thought for a long time. "I want you to find me several different things that I can use to give you a beating. Do not interrupt, not one word!" He shouted as she opened her mouth to protest. "Not one! I want you to bring me at least five things for me to use. Next, I want you to find something I can use to tie you up. Nylons might be good. Or silk scarves. Then I want you to pack enough food and clothes for a week at the cabin for both of us. Next week, when we get back, and after any bruises from your punishment fade," hearing this Sally paled, "I will take you to the doctor. You need to be tested for pregnancy and diseases." His voice broke, "God! You little fool! Don't you think at all? You have heard of AIDS, haven't you? Wasn't it bad enough to lose your mother? Do I have to worry about losing you too?"

Sally was sobbing with fear and with the harsh realization that she was getting dangerously close to losing her father's love and being tossed out of her home. She couldn't manage a coherent word.

Matt went on, "I'll go talk to what's his name now. Pray that I don't kill him."

Paul was waiting downstairs, dressed now and visibly upset. He was shaking and still somehow defiant. Matt looked at the insolent young man. He was Matt's worst nightmare. He was the worst nightmare of any young girl's father. He was slender and good-looking, in a teenage way. He had long, straight brown hair with angry brown eyes, tight jeans and a torn T-shirt with some heavy metal band named on it. There was a tattoo showing at the bottom of the sleeve of his T-shirt. Matt realized that he had half expected the young man to run.

Matt could barely stand to look at Paul when he spoke to him. "I want you to know exactly what's going to happen to Sally, all because of you. I only wish I could do the same thing to you, but I can't. I can keep you away from her in the future. I can probably get you put in prison, if that's what it takes to do it. You have heard of drug laws? Drinking underage? Giving alcohol to a minor? Statutory rape?" He paused, "Sally will be physically punished for each of her recent actions: lying, drinking, smoking, skipping school, using cocaine, marijuana and sex, unprotected sex. Are you ready to raise a child? Are you ready to die for a few minutes of thrills? Are you ready to risk her life for your fun?" He wasn't yelling, not quite, but it was every bit as effective.

"Next, you'll tell me you love her. You idiot," he sneered. "Kids your age and Sally's age are dying from unprotected sex. They die from drug use. And don't forget, the largest cause of death for teens is drinking and driving! From my point of view, you might as well have picked up a gun and tried to kill my daughter."

"Hey! I'm clean. No diseases. And girls don't get pregnant every time, do they?" Paul protested. "And I can hold my alcohol."

"Have you been AIDS tested?" Matt asked.

"I don't need to," Paul replied.

"Jackass." Matt pulled in his temper with an almost palpable effort. "Do you think any of the people with AIDS thought they were going to get it? Or did they think it wouldn't happen to them? Do you think that the teenage birth rate is so high because all those girls wanted to have a baby? Some maybe, but all of them? Do you think that all those kids who die in drunk driving accidents knew they would die? I know, as sure as I live and breathe, that at some point in their lives every one of them told somebody that they could hold their liquor. Don't you know that it's not always the other guy? Sometimes it's you." He stopped. "Get out. Now. Before I kill you."

"Wait!" Paul said. "Please sir, don't hurt Sally!"

He worked his courage up. It was the first hint Matt could find that the boy really cared for Sally.

"Please! Punish me instead! Just please don't hurt Sally."

Incredibly there were tears streaming down his face. "And please sir, let us keep on seeing each other. I do love her."

Matt stood there and looked at the boy. Thinking. It went against every instinct he had, the very idea set his teeth on edge but he knew that he would have to do as they asked and let them keep seeing each other. He was smart enough to know that if he tried to stop Sally from seeing Paul completely, she would really rebel. If he let her see the boy, they would think he was giving them a major privilege. Besides, after Matt got through with him, Paul wouldn't dare take any chances with Sally.

Finally he spoke. "I won't change my mind about the punishment I'm going to give Sally. But, if you will agree to submit voluntarily to the same punishment, and let's be clear, I mean a very harsh beating, and if you will agree to follow the rules that I set without question, I will let you see Sally. Of course you can only see her in my presence, and only for as long as you continue to follow all my rules. Agreed?"

At Paul's speechless nod, Matt continued, "You will drive yourself up to the cabin, following my truck. Go home. Pack for at least a week. Do you live with your parents?"

The boy spoke. "I live with my mother. My Dad left us about four years ago." He swallowed hard and paused before continuing, "Please don't tell her about this. I know I've done things to hurt her but this will be too much for her. She's had a hard time with me since Dad left."

"Do you expect to get any sympathy with that line?" Matt asked coldly.

"No sir," Paul whispered, "not for me but for my mother… "

"Have your mother call me. I need to talk to her before we leave, then you get your butt back here in two hours! Got it?" Matt chose not to answer his plea.

Paul nodded, "Yes sir." He gathered his courage. "Sir, what are you going to tell my Mom?"

"Whatever it takes to get her permission to give you the beating of your life," Matt said. "I'll probably threaten to have you put in jail. Of course, I will have to mention the drinking, drugs and sex."

"If I can get Mom to give her permission without having you tell her all of it, would that be okay?" Paul asked.

"Not completely. It wouldn't be honest, but I could tone it down. I also want a confession from you. In your own words. Write out what you and Sally were doing, drugs and all, along with a statement that you are willing to accept physical punishment from me. Now go!" As Paul headed for the door Matt added, "When you get back from the cabin I want you to go get tested for all S.T.D.'s"

"What are S.T.D.'s?"

"Sexually Transmitted Diseases, you dumb ass."

In two hours, Matt had suitcases for himself and for Sally loaded on the back of his truck. He had approved of the items that Sally had selected for her punishment, filled a cooler with food and the perishables from the refrigerator, and turned off the lights. He had also had a long talk on the phone with Paul's mother. At first, Paul's mother wanted to blame the whole incident on Sally, but she finally admitted that the boy needed to learn a lesson. By the end of the conversation she had agreed to back Matt up every step of the way, and promised that there would be some changes in Paul's life when the boy got back from the cabin.

"I don't care if he is eighteen, he's going to have to learn to live by the rules!" Paul's mother vowed.

"For his own good, as much as anything else," Matt agreed.

He and Sally were waiting outside for Paul. When the boy arrived, they all got into their vehicles and started out.

It was not a cheery ride up to the cabin; Matt barely had his anger under control and Sally was torn between fear, pleading, and defiance. Paul followed in his own car, all the while wanting to turn around and yet felt that he had to go on.

As Matt and Sally passed a bus station about halfway up to the cabin, Matt said, "This is it. This is the bottom line: If you and Paul don't go along with everything that I do and say this week, without a single word of complaint, that bus station is where I will leave you. I won't let you come back home until you agree to live by the rules. Of course, Paul won't be just left off, he'll be arrested. Do you understand?"

"Daddy, would you really kick me out?" She stared at him, wide eyed.

"I don't want to," Matt answered firmly. "I don't want to beat you. I don't even want to be strict with you. I also don't want to see you pregnant, dead of a drug overdose, or a car crash, or sick with AIDS. In other words, if you want to destroy yourself I don't want to see it and I sure won't help you to do it. If you want to have a future, get a good education, and live a long, happy life then I will help you all I can. I will do anything to make that happen."

"Daddy, I love you, I'll try to do what you want." She was almost whispering.

"I love you too, sweetheart, and I promise not to spend so much time at the office in the future, okay?" He felt a little better about his daughter already.

"But I'm still in major hairy trouble, right?" She felt compelled to check.

"Right." There was no mercy in Matt's tone.

They made one stop along the way, outside a saddle and feed store. Matt called Paul over. "You got any money, kid?" Paul nodded, puzzled. "Then go into the store and buy a riding crop, 18 inches to 2 feet long, and not one of those wimpy little thin ones. Get a heavy crop, boy, something that will hurt." Paul went pale but he obeyed, reluctantly, without saying a word. There was a slight hitch in his step when Matt added, "Oh, and a leather strap too."

When they had pulled up in front of the small cabin and parked, Matt got out of his truck and walked back to Paul's car. He told the young man to go into the upstairs bedroom and work on the paper he had agreed to write. He was going to deal with Sally first.

"You won't," Paul paused for a moment, "hurt her, will you?" Paul asked. "It was all my fault," he admitted. "I was being really stupid and ignoring the risks, thinking only of myself, just like you said. I even risked getting her into trouble with you."

"She's my daughter, I love her," Matt replied. "Of course I won't do anything to injure her or to really hurt her. And I know very well how much you had to do with the trouble she's in. I was your age once, but I don't remember being as dumb as you are. I'm glad to hear you admit it." It was the first sign that the young man had any sense of morals or responsibility at all.

"I'm going to get it worse, aren't I?" he asked Matt quietly.

"How can I put this? You are bigger, stronger and older and most of all, I don't love you one damn bit. You know I had a talk with your mother over the phone. She sounds like a sweet woman and I know you've put her through hell. I told her what you had done, and how I planned to treat the matter. I will also have the written paper that you agreed to give me. In other words, I have permission from your mother and from you to give you a harsh beating. The good news is that if I'm satisfied with the severity of the beating your mother won't call your Dad, so you won't have to face any more trouble from your father when you get home. But you might want to kiss your car good-bye. The registration slip's in your mother's name." He flashed a killer smile at Paul. "Come on inside and we'll talk it over."

"What happens if I don't?" His defiance was only partly an act.

"In that case, you'll never see Sally again. I will press any legal charges that I can think of against you. Your Mom will report her car as being stolen. And, if your Dad gets his hands on you, you'll probably get the beating anyway!" That deadly smile flashed again. "In other words, no matter what you do your ass is grass."

As Matt walked back to his truck he found that Sally had unloaded the clothes and food, and she sat waiting in the living room of the cabin. She was terrified, sitting there looking at the items that were to be used in her punishment. Following her father's orders, she had put the stuff on the coffee table.

There was a long, wooden spoon; a thick, rubber soled sandal;

her father's heavy, leather belt; and a natural bristle hairbrush; Matt added two items to this collection, the crop that he had ordered Paul to buy, and a rough pine switch that he had cut himself.

Matt said, "Paul, go on up there and write that paper I asked for. Please don't let any screams or noises that you might hear distract you, and don't come down those stairs until I tell you to." The boy left the room, turning back at the foot of the stairs to look at Sally.

"Go!" Matt commanded.

Paul went on up the stairs.

Sally was still sitting nervously on the sofa. "Which of these things are," she stopped and swallowed several times, then went on, "are you going to use on me, Daddy?"

"Sit down Sally, don't be so eager." She made a choking sound but he continued, "I notice that you only found four things."

"No, there's five," Sally protested. "The fifth thing you can use to beat me is your hand."

"Good thinking," Matt said. "Okay, let me explain. The way I see it you have seven different punishments coming. One for each of the things you've been doing lately. There's skipping school, lying, smoking, drinking, using marijuana, snorting cocaine and having sex. Sex without taking any responsibility for the outcome. You are going to get seven separate punishments. You have a choice to either take them all today or one a day like vitamins, for a week. If it were me, I would personally take all I could today and get it over with. Then, you and Paul will have some rules set down for you."

"I'm scared, Daddy, what if I can't take it?" Her voice shook and she had tears in her eyes.

"That's why I'm going to tie you. You won't have a choice, no chance to struggle and no one to hear you scream. Except Paul, and I like the idea of him hearing you scream. It will give him an idea of what's in store for him. Enough delay; take off your clothes from your waist down, except your underwear. NOW!" She did it, moving slowly, until her father added, "If it takes you too long, I'll add an extra punishment. I'm sure I can find a wooden hanger or a ping-pong paddle around here." It was truly amazing how fast she got undressed.

Matt sat on a large pine chair and pulled her down across his knees. He positioned her so that her forehead was almost touching the floor. Her hands and long blond hair, of course, were resting on the floor. He pulled her underwear down and without any warning he began to spank her backside with hard, heavy blows. He was a man of some strength and the blows were given with some force behind them. It was the first time she had ever been spanked.

Each time his large hand crashed down on her bare butt it made a loud sound. Crack! Each blow produced a muffled gasp from Sally. After laying about a dozen hits on each side alternately, he put four in a row on the left side, much harder than any before, then he did the same to the right side. Sally screamed and began to cry.

"Shut up!" Matt commanded. "And relax your butt. NOW!"

Against her will, she obeyed. After four more harsh hits on each side he stopped spanking her bottom.

"Get up and sit right here on this wooden chair." She started to pull her underpants up. "Leave your pants where they are."

She obeyed, red-faced and crying.

Matt walked to the table then came back over. He used the scarf to tie her hands together in front of her. He pulled a footstool to the center of the room and ordered her to kneel over it. He used one scarf to tie her hands to the stool legs and another scarf to tie her feet.

"You've had one punishment, are you ready for another?" he asked sternly.

"Daddy." She was sobbing, her tone was protesting, almost pleading.

"The only acceptable answer is, 'Yes daddy, please punish me.'" His voice was soft and but intimidating.

"Daddy, punish, please," she managed, choking.

"Close enough."

He picked up the wooden spoon and began to use it. He hit her with sharp, hard, even strokes landing on both buttocks at once. He wasn't as harsh with her as he had been with his hands, but the way her butt felt, she didn't realize it. The concave nature of the spoon made the most fascinating oval bruises with slightly pale centers. After about a dozen strokes he gave her two sharp reminders, harder than the others then he stopped. He sat down and with a shaking hand that Sally couldn't see, ran his fingers through his short brown hair.

"You'll have to wait a bit if you want the third one today, love." Matt sounded exhausted.

"Daddy!" Tears were streaming down her face.

"You do remember the only acceptable answer, don't you?" It was a quiet reminder.

"Please, don't make me wait tied up like this, please just punish me NOW!" Sally was scared, in pain and in an uncomfortable position.

Matt picked up the hairbrush and gave her two spankings with it. First, he gave her a dozen blows on each cheek separately, hard but not extreme. Next, he used the side with bristles, forming little blood blisters. She squirmed and tossed her head, yelling at each SWAT of the hairbrush.

He paused for a few minutes to let the pain soak in to her bright, red buttocks and her brain.

After a while he said, "Ready girl?"

Sally tried to answer but she could only nod. Matt used the sandal with the rubber soul next. It stung quite a bit and made her butt bright red. He really wasn't hitting her all that hard. It wasn't necessary. All that was really necessary was for Sally to think he was being extremely severe. He hit her ten stinging blows on each side of her butt. SMACK!

He untied her. "Get up girl, go sit in the chair and rest."

"I'd rather not sit down," she managed to get out between her sobs.

"It wasn't a question, sit down now!" Matt barked.

She did it without further protest. Tears were streaming down her face. About half an hour later he ordered her to lay face down on the heavy, pine coffee table.

He picked up the riding crop and asked her, "Ready?"

She nodded.

He hit her about a dozen slashing cuts with the riding crop. When he had finished, he told her to remain in place. He went up the stairs. As soon as he left the room she stood up and began to softly rub her aching buttocks. She kept a close watch on the stairs.

"How's the paper coming?" he asked Paul.

He took the handwritten paper from the boy, looked it over and saw that it was finished. It was simple and honest, taking all responsibility for his actions.

"Sir, how's Sally?" Paul ventured.

"She's in pain but she'll be okay. It's almost over." Matt grinned and turned to leave with the parting shot, "For her."

When Matt got back downstairs he made some coffee and waited for a short time before the punishment started again. He gave her about twenty with the belt, trying to ignore her screams. What Sally didn't realize was that except for the spanking with his hand, Matt hadn't used very hard force in his blows. He wanted to punish her and make a permanent impression on her, not kill her.

Then the leather strap. When he finished with the strap, he helped her to stand on shaky feet and told her to sit down again in the wooden chair. This time she did it without a word of protest. Tears were streaming down her face. After a while she noticed the tears in her father's brown eyes and realized that her father was crying too. The sight of her proud, usually gentle father with tears on his cheeks, tears that she caused, really shook her up. She made up her mind to do whatever he said, if she could. It was hard to follow orders because she was in so much pain.

When he was ready Matt picked up the rough switch and gave the order. "Stand up Sally, turn around, bend over and grab onto the seat of the chair with both hands. Whatever you do, don't take your hands off the chair. Stay in position and take it until I tell you it's over, understand?"

"Yes Daddy, please, punish me," she whispered.

She mustered all her courage and did as she was told. Matt hit her as hard as he could across both cheeks of her buttocks causing her to scream loudly and take her hands off the chair, straightening up.

Immediately she realized her mistake and said, "I'm sorry Daddy!"

Using all her courage she bent over again and gripped the chair. "I'll do better next time."

Matt realized that she had finally submitted. Her defiance was gone. In its place was the will to obey. No matter what it cost her in terms of pain.

"Stand up Sally, you've had enough," he finally relented.

"You mean all I had to do was scream and stand up for you to quit?" She didn't quite understand.

"No silly Sally, you idiot, all you had to do was show enough courage and obedience to apologize and bend back over. After a hit as hard as the last one, it took quite a bit of effort."

"Is it really over?" She wanted and needed the reassurance of hearing him say it.

"Yes, it's over. Go to the back bedroom and lock the door. Do not come out until I tell you to. Paul will need his privacy. Take some ice and a cool cloth. It may ease your behind. We'll talk later, all three of us, and we might be able to work out some ground rules that we can all agree on."

"You're really going to beat Paul?" she asked in wide-eyed curiosity.

"Yes." He was firm.

"As hard as you did me?" Her expression was incredulous.

"Probably harder," her father replied, grinning, "I don't love him."

"And I can't watch?" she asked curiously.

"NO!" he answered sternly. "GO!"

"Darn!" she said as she left to get some ice and a cool cloth.

Hearing that remark, Matt laughed for the first time that day and thought to himself, *"Bloodthirsty brat!"*

When she had gone into the bedroom and locked the door, Matt tidied up the living room. He put away all the things he had used to punish Sally except the brush, the riding crop and the switch. He went upstairs.

"Next!" he called to Paul. "The sooner you get in here the sooner it'll all be over, except for the pain of course."

Once again the smile appeared, the killer smile, as he thought of the target. This time he would enjoy his chore.

Before the punishment started Matt said to Paul, "If you want to know how hard this is going to hurt, or how I feel about you, just sit there for a minute and think. It's a few years in the future. You have a bright beautiful daughter. She's all that you love in the world. Then a young smartass gets her to do things that could kill her. He starts her on drinking, drugs and casual sex with no protection. If it doesn't kill her it could ruin her future. You know that he doesn't mean her any harm, in fact he thinks he loves her, but you also know that thousands of young girls have their lives ruined or ended by the things he wants her to do with him. Think. What would you do to the guy?"

Matt walked away. He went into the kitchen and got a beer. He let the kid sit and think, hoping it would do some good, maybe even as much as the beating that would follow.

After about fifteen minutes or so he asked Paul, "Well, what would you do to the punk?"

"Honestly? I'd kill him." The boy looked pale and scared. "I would." He looked down at the floor but after a few seconds he looked up. "But please sir, don't kill me."

"So you do accept my right to punish you?" At the boy's nod, he went on, "Drop your pants and bend over. Take your underwear down too. And you'd better not move! Remember not to yell too much or Sally will hear you. You wouldn't want her to think that you're a coward. I'm going to use the crop first, then the brush, then the switch, and yes I WILL hit you harder than I hit Sally. Just be glad that I don't beat you from the front."

At that remark Paul's face turned ashen and his knees buckled.

When Paul was bent over, holding the seat of the chair like Matt had told him to, the beating began. Matt used the crop and he used it with a lot more force than he had with his daughter; after all, this was technically a grown man and from a father's point of view he more than deserved it!

The blows got harder and harder the more he went on, landing sometimes on one cheek or the other, and sometimes on both. One or two lashes of the crop even landed on his legs. Almost all the blows caused immediate welts. Paul struggled to keep quiet, but he finally surrendered to the pain. He came out with a series of earsplitting yells. Matt gave the boy about three dozen lashes with the crop; almost each one was harder than the one before. Finally he quit and sat down.

"Sit down, Paul we're going to take a break before I use the hairbrush. I hope you don't mind?"

Paul seated himself very gingerly on the hard wooden chair and replied, "We can wait forever if you want, in fact I'd prefer it."

Matt secretly admired his aplomb.

"Sally didn't try to get out of any of it, and I used seven different things on her," Matt chided him.

"You love her," Paul said softly. "I'll bet that she didn't catch it this hard, even with seven things. Besides, I'm not trying to get out of it, just to be agreeable."

"Okay Mr. Agreeable, assume the position once again." Matt picked up the hairbrush.

"THAT! How much can it hurt?" Paul was almost laughing.

He stopped laughing when Matt brought the hard bristles down violently on his bare ass in a series of very hard blows all on his left cheek. There was not very much sound but each one landed on a spot that was already sore, and each one caused severe pain. After about twenty he moved his attention to the right cheek.

When he was done, again he gave the quiet command, "Sit down Paul." Then he asked, "How do you feel?"

"Are you nuts? I feel terrible. I also feel guilty that Sally is feeling any pain because of me." Paul looked at Matt. "Or do you think I'm just saying that to try to get you to go a little easier on me?"

"It doesn't matter because it didn't work." Matt looked at Paul, weighing his opinion of him.

He wouldn't admit it, but by now he had come to a grudging respect for the boy. Paul was taking his punishment like a man. Matt knew from talking to Paul's mother that the boy had never even been spanked before.

"But yes, just for the record, I think that you do feel a little guilt, maybe even a lot. I just don't think that you've really learned anything yet. I hope you do. Whether you are going out with my daughter or someone else. Even if it's just for yourself, I want you to learn to think of the consequences of your actions. You see, I don't want anything to ruin your life. I'm surprised at myself, shocked even, but I seem to care about getting through to you, one way or another."

"Sir," Paul said quietly, "I want to tell you something. I know it won't make any difference as far as my punishment, but," he looked down for a moment then he met Matt's eyes, "you got home just in time. We hadn't... I mean, she's still a virgin."

Matt closed his eyes for a minute, relieved.

He looked at Paul. "Thanks. But, and don't take this as permission to do anything, sex wasn't my biggest fear. Understand?" The boy nodded. "So stand up and bend over."

Paul did as instructed without any protest, but it was very clear that he was reluctant. Matt noticed that the door to the back bedroom was slightly opened, and thought he saw a trace of movement when he looked at the door. He smiled to himself.

Matt used the rough heavy pine switch on Paul's legs and ass with loud swishing strokes that he laid on slowly. Each one was a separate assault on the young man's senses. Each one whistled as the switch was swung. Each one caused him to yell. Each one caused some blood to flow because of the roughness of the switch. After about twenty or so strokes, Paul broke down and began to sob like a baby. Shortly after that the whipping was finally stopped. Matt told Paul to go upstairs to the loft.

After the boy left, Matt picked up in the living room so that all traces of the terrible punishments were gone. He got some antibiotic ointment and an ice pack and took them up to Paul.

"Here. I know that I drew blood in quite a few places, so take care of yourself. Just lie there and rest, okay?" Matt held out the supplies surprising Paul with his gentleness; he seemed to harbor no ill will towards the boy.

"I'm going to call your mother," Matt told the boy, "and tell her I think you deserve a chance to change your ways before she punishes you any further."

Paul was almost speechless but he managed to say, "Thank you sir, I'll do my best to see that you don't regret it."

"I know I said that you and Sally and I would talk tomorrow and set some ground rules for when you two see each other but when I told your mother about it she wanted to be in on the discussion. I thought it would be a good idea for her to come up tomorrow and join us. Do you have any objections?"

"I really don't feel like facing her right now," Paul said, "because I finally realize just how much trouble I've caused her, but I don't object."

Matt went down and checked on his daughter. "How's it going?"

"I'm sore, but feeling better," she replied quietly.

"I know you peeked while I was beating Paul, you defiant little twerp," Matt said gently. "I thought you were going to be obedient from now on."

"I said I'd be obedient, not a saint," Sally protested, giving her father a mischievous look.

"Good. Saints are all right, but I want more from my daughter. I don't want you to be perfect, just to take responsibility for the results of your actions. Got it?" Matt hugged her.

"Got it," she paused and looked at her father. "I know that I deserved what I got, but Daddy, will you forgive me?"

"Of course I forgive you, I love you. Rest now unless you want to come out and watch TV with me." He gave her another squeeze.

Matt kissed her forehead, and then went out to the living room to have another beer and watch football. Before long Sally came out to watch the game with him.

"How's Paul?" she asked. "From the bedroom it looked horrible and sounded barbaric! Great! You really had him yelling!"

The two of them heard a strange choking sound from upstairs.

"Gee, I'm glad you thought it was great," Paul called down. "I sure didn't!"

"Eavesdropper!" Sally laughed, then turned her attention back to her father.

Matt replied to Sally's original statement, ignoring the interruption, "Barbaric? What a word, are you reading those bodice-ripper novels again? Ferocious little wench aren't you? I'll go up and check on him again at half time. Let's leave him alone a little while." He turned to watch the play just as the wide receiver dropped what should have been an easy catch. "Damn! That guy couldn't even catch a cold!"

"It's just that Paul pushed me into a lot of it," she explained her blood lust. "I know that I am responsible for making my own decisions, but he is older and all, right? So he wasn't innocent either."

"Right, he's at a young and stupid age. I wasn't any saint at eighteen either." Matt kissed her on the forehead. "Let's forget it for tonight and talk tomorrow when his Mom gets here."

"Easy for you to say, you can sit down!" She curled up in her father's arms then yelled, "What idiots! The jerks always fumble on the ten-yard line."

Just then the two heard a voice from above.

"What's the score?" Paul asked.

"Come down and watch. There are sodas in the fridge," Matt invited. "Just don't bet with my daughter."

"Because I'd corrupt her?" Paul asked cautiously, entering the room.

His face was pale and his eyes were red, but he seemed composed. Matt's grudging respect for the boy grew.

Matt gave the boy a genuine smile for the first time. "No, because she always wins."

Bright and early the next day, Matt and Paul went to town. Matt had arranged to meet Paul's mother, Joan, at the local hamburger stand and lead her through the back roads to his remote cabin. Matt was surprised when Joan turned out to be a very attractive woman of about forty. She had a trim shape, well-styled auburn hair with worried brown eyes. He stood off to one side and watched her as she greeted her son. She seemed torn between the desire to hug Paul and the urge to strangle him.

Paul stood beside Matt, watching his mother uncertainly. "Hi, Mom."

"How are you Paul?" she asked with maternal concern.

"I'm okay." He gave her a shy half-smile. "I'm sorry, I'm really sorry for all the trouble I seem to give you lately."

"You *have* been a pain in the butt, but I love you Paul." She hugged him gently. "Can we start over?"

"Sure Mom, as long as you don't mention pain and butt in the same sentence," Paul joked weakly. "I love you too."

"Did he hurt you? Really, physically hurt you?" She glanced over at Matt.

"Hell, yes," Paul answered readily, "but I'll survive. I deserved it."

"Are you bruised?" she asked.

Paul blushed looking at his mother, "You'll never know."

Joan just stood there looking at him. She raised one eyebrow, inquisitively. "When we get back to the cabin, you're going to show me."

"Aw Mom, please don't make me show you. Please." Seeing her smile, he relaxed. "By the way have you met Matt?"

Joan turned to greet Matt and met his eyes for the first time. She silently noted his dark blond hair and his deep brown eyes. His face was worn but not haggard, and he had great bone structure. He was about her age, fit and trim, but not too lean. He was handsome, indeed! There was an instant reaction.

Matt reached out and they shook hands murmuring polite greetings to each other. Paul looked from one to the other several times with a slight grin on his face feeling temporarily forgotten. Finally he cleared his throat.

"Hey, I don't want to interrupt you two while you're still shaking hands." He looked at his watch. "It's only been five minutes. When does hand shaking become hand holding?" he asked with exaggerated innocence.

"Paul, you can drive your mother's car back to the cabin, Joan's riding with me." Matt didn't even turn his head to look at the boy.

"Why am I not surprised?" Paul muttered as he got into the car, trying not to wince as he slid his still sore buttocks behind the wheel.

Much to Paul's dismay and total humiliation his mother insisted on seeing the marks left from the beating Matt had given him. Afterwards she found Matt in the kitchen with his daughter.

"Can I speak to your father alone?" she asked Sally.

Sally nodded and went outside. Joan turned to Matt. "I never thought I'd say this to anyone but thank you for beating my son. I don't know how he got so far out of control." She met Matt's eyes. "And he's told me some of the things you've said to him too. Thank you."

"I think he'll be a fine man someday when he learns to take responsibility for his actions," Matt admitted. "There's a lot of good in that boy."

Surprisingly, the rest of the week passed pleasantly. The two adults tried to tread the thin line between advising the teens and lecturing them. Sally and Paul were both on their good behavior, but they both had a hard time trying to resist teasing their respective parents about the sparks flying between them.

After a few days, Paul and Sally came back from a hike and found Matt and Joan in the living room kissing passionately.

"Can I ask a question, Daddy?" Sally asked, ignoring her

father's discomfiture at having the kids walk in.

"Sure, brat. What's up?" Matt knew that impish look.

"Why is it okay for you and Paul's Mom to be doing it... I mean, kissing, ah heck, you know, and not Paul and me?"

"Because Joan and I are adults. That's not just a matter of age, but it involves respect and self-control. Neither one of us is trying to use drugs, or alcohol, or even persuasion to push the other into doing something irresponsible, something we'll regret. And for the record young lady, we were not doing it. We were just kissing. Kissing a lot, but just kissing. If and when we make love, I can guarantee you one thing: neither you nor Paul will walk in on it," Matt said firmly.

"I'll second that," Joan said smiling. "Having you two find us kissing was bad enough."

She looked at Sally cautiously. "Does it bother you, honey? That your father and I are interested in each other, I mean. I know you lost your mother fairly recently."

"No. It's okay, I guess, as long as... " Sally paused, uncertain.

"What, honey?" Joan prompted.

"As long as he still has time for me," Sally blurted.

Matt reached up and pulled Sally down onto his lap, hugging her. "I promise I'll never neglect you again. I love you." He looked up. "How do you feel about me seeing your mother, Paul?"

"Just treat her okay and I won't complain," Paul said. "She deserves to be treated better than she has by the men in her life. Including me."

That night, feeling as if they had the seal of approval, Matt and Joan made love long into the night. They were both passionate and giving people. Before the summer was over they were married. Paul and Sally teased their folks when Joan had her baby only seven months after the wedding.

"Maybe I should get out the horsewhip," Paul remarked deadpan. "It seems like you got my mother in trouble before the wedding."

"But I did right by her, Paul. I was and am taking full

responsibility for my actions," Matt defended himself. "Besides, you got a new sister out of the deal."

"And a new father too. Right?" He grinned at the man who had become his best friend.

"Right."

Paul and Sally slowly settled into their new relationship as stepbrother and sister. All signs of teenage romance disappeared.

At least it seemed that way until Paul finished college and Sally turned eighteen, and then without a word they eloped. Young love usually fades but sometimes young love lasts forever.

A father's love can be a real tough challenge with a rebellious teen; this is a serious, but I felt necessary story. Like a harsh spanking can be necessary, or so many people believe. For myself, I think a spanking is just good old-fashioned fun!

Seven

Personal: The First Time

What do you say to an outrageous suggestion from the man you love? What if it's something he really wants? What do you do? How much do you trust him? How afraid are you? Do you secretly enjoy the shivers running down your spine? Definitely auto-biographical and mostly true, only the names have been changed, as they say. Of course, I also changed the description and the woman's figure. Heck, if I can't diet myself into a raving beauty, I can at least write myself as one, can't I?

"You want to do *what?*" Ann's voice came as a surprised shriek and she began to pace around the room on her long, slender legs.

"Stop pacing and stand still, you'll wear a hole in the rug," Jerry said wryly.

Jerry was her best friend and wanted to be her lover. He pulled her into a warm hug and kissed her gently before he continued calmly and firmly, repeating again the outrageous statement he had greeted her with when he had first arrived.

"All I said was, I want to spank you." Then he added a single word, implacably, "Hard."

"*What?*" She pulled back in his embrace just enough to look up into his eyes. In her surprise, it was the only word she could manage to say. For once in her life Ann was speechless.

He gave her a mischievous grin and a wink, his twinkling brown eyes full of laughter, then he spoke slowly and with exaggerated patience. "I want to raise and lower my hand, bringing it down quickly and repeatedly on your bare buttocks, starting slowly, and not very hard. I want to hear the slap of my palm on your bare skin and feel the warmth of your skin as it

99

begins to turn pink. Then I want to increase the speed and the force of the blows, causing your buttocks to turn bright red and hot, and causing you to feel a little stinging, then some real smarting, and finally pain. Really," another grin and wink, "you must have heard of it before. It is a practice commonly used on misbehaving children. There's even a debate as to whether or not it's child abuse."

"I am not a misbehaving child!" she said with force.

Jerry just grinned as he looked at her, noting her full breasts and round bottom. He said, "I know, baby. Believe me, I know."

Her eyes got as large as saucers and her jaw dropped; she was nearly speechless. She was more astonished than she had ever been before. She managed to get out one more incredulous word.

"Why?" She stopped. She swallowed hard before finally continuing, "What's the thrill for you? And what's in it for me?"

"I'll tell you what's in it for you first: Well, there's some pain, maybe lots of pain, and also heat, fear, embarrassment, loss of control, submission, the feeling of helplessness, of having your fate in another's hands, and of being an object, but a cherished object." He paused and gave her a lingering and appraising look, taking in her flushed face, her heaving breasts and her wide blue-green eyes. God! She was gorgeous! "It may be that you'll also get sexual pleasure from it. Many people do."

He continued, "Why do I want to do it? Because I love you. I love your round, firm butt. I want to make it sting, really sting. I want to see it turn bright red and be able to put my hands on it to feel how hot I made it."

Jerry paused again trying to find words to explain. "We have a weird relationship. After all the time we've spent together and how much we're in love, you still won't have sex with me because I'm married. Okay, that's fair. I don't like it, in fact I hate it, but it's fair. That means we're in love but we don't have sex. Any form of sex. You refuse to suck me off or to let me sodomize you, and I respect your reasons for that. I'm disappointed and horny as hell but that's your decision, so that's how it is. You have strong beliefs about being with a married man even though you love me, and even though my wife and I are probably going to be divorced soon."

He paused, thinking before he continued, "So a spanking, while it's sexy and kinky isn't actually sex, and it's something I've always wanted to try that I've never done with my wife or with any other woman. It would be our little secret, ours alone, something that's special and unique only to us. Remember how you told me once that your parents had never spanked you? It would be just me. I'd be the only one. My hand making your butt burn and turn red. I'd be in control of your pleasure and your pain. You would have to give me your complete trust. If I can't have your body for sex, I can at least have your trust."

"I do like the idea of sharing something special with you. Something that you have never shared with another woman, and I've never shared with another man." She continued, "And you do have my complete trust, you know that, but why does it have to be a spanking? I mean be real, Bud, this is the nineties. I'm a liberated woman. This is not just out of date, it's positively medieval!" She left his arms to resume pacing around the room agitated and puzzled, trying to ignore the quivering and the little spot of warmth in the pit of her stomach, the slight tingling on her buttocks.

She realized that her breathing was getting faster and her breasts felt strange, heavy and tight. Were these feelings the first hints of something? Fear? Excitement? Arousal?

Fear, she told herself firmly, it must be fear. Even as the thought crossed her mind, she knew she was lying to herself. She could never fear Jerry, not really.

"So what if it is medieval? I've seen the books you always leave lying around, all you ever read are historical romances. You are pretty medieval yourself, or at least your fantasies are," he said firmly. "Besides, you really don't have a choice in this. I'm going to do it no matter what you say."

"I'll fight." She raised her chin defiantly.

"I'll enjoy the fight, and I'll win," he said with a touch of male bravado. "You can't stop me."

"I'll scream," she tried again.

"I'll gag you," he countered.

"I'll report it to the police," she finally threatened.

"But not until after it's all over, and think about how you would feel telling the police, or a judge, or a jury about how you were spanked. And consider this: you've said no, and rightly so, so many times to so many things. Say yes this once. Just this once do something for me, even if it doesn't seem to be something you'd want to do. You may even enjoy it." It was as close to begging as he would ever come.

Ann looked at him silently and considered the crazy idea. She noticed the slight thinning of his straight brown hair. It had been thick when they first met. Had it really been that long ago? She thought back, remembering how their relationship first began.

It started out as a simple joking and teasing friendship between co-workers. Jerry became her own personal pest at work, but in a fun way. He drove her nuts but he was always there to support, comfort and assist her. He would comfort her, then make a clumsy pass with a laugh. He would walk her to her car when she got off work at nearly midnight, wait until she was safely locked in with her window down part of the way so they could talk, and just as she rolled her window up he would make a grab at her breasts. If he'd really wanted to grab her she always knew he wouldn't wait for her to roll up her car window. She always drove off with a laugh.

Then he quit work. He had another job; it paid more and offered him a better future. Ann missed him terribly since he had certainly livened things up at the company. Without him, her workdays seemed duller and longer. The only bright spot for her was that she no longer had to fight herself from crossing a boundary with a married man. Pest that he was, Jerry had been getting more and more tempting.

After not seeing Jerry for over six months he became her neighbor, purely by accident. Jerry didn't know, couldn't know, that Ann lived on the same block when he and his wife bought their first house. Ann always laughed to herself as she thought of the mixed blessing of having her friendly pest from work move into a house almost next door to hers. She would never forget the day when he walked over to her as she was getting her groceries out of her car.

"Is this your house?" he asked, laughter and joy on his round olive brown face.

"Jerry! What the heck are you doing here?" Ann was surprised and glad to see him.

"My wife and I just moved into that house," he gestured to a light brown house a few houses down from hers.

"Oh my God! Mr. 'Sexual-Harassment-from-work' is living on my block," she teased him. "There goes the neighborhood."

Jerry grinned with delight, "Now you can be harassed at home on your own time. Just think of all the advantages, the possibilities, the... ah... "

"Neighbors, your wife," Ann countered.

Although Jerry and his wife didn't stay in that house very long, while they were living there the friendship between Jerry and Ann deepened. The flirting got heavier and the companionship grew. He would come to see her after he got off work around midnight just to visit and relax. It was a much needed companionship for both of them.

Ann had left her job and she was now tied to the house caring for her ailing mother, and Jerry really hated to go straight home from work to a sleeping wife and no one to talk to. And boy did they talk; they talked about everything from the latest movies to sports, politics, religion and even some things so personal that Ann had never discussed them with her closest girlfriends.

Even in the early days the love was there, silently growing. They didn't really take it any farther than friendship until after Ann's mother died, and then for their own reasons, reasons that had nothing to do with Ann, Jerry and his wife decided to separate.

Soon, Jerry came over even more often. Gradually Ann and Jerry began to kiss and fool around like high school kids making out on their parent's sofa. He was always trying to get into Ann's clothes. Somehow he almost always succeeded, at least partially. Ann began to feel like she was in a love affair with an octopus. He would kiss her and tease her constantly. She felt his fingers gently squeeze her nipples or slide in and out of her moist vagina. Sometimes those magic fingers would even tease her tight anus. Even then she resisted actual intercourse because in her heart she still believed he was a married man. Now they were at a turning point in their relationship.

Ann realized that this was the turning point; his request to give her occasional sexual spankings meant a lot to him. In fact, she secretly wondered how he had gotten the nerve to ask her.

So she considered the idea and thought of the love she felt for him. She thought of the long years of self-denial for both of them and his patience. Surely there was real love behind his monumental patience?

She also thought of the fact that he had never asked her to do anything just for him. Oh, he wanted her to have sex with him. He was horny every time she had ever seen him. He asked for sex but he had never asked her to go against her principles, and he had never insisted or threatened. She thought long and hard and she weighed her options because as always with her lover, the choice was really hers. No matter what he said.

What he didn't realize was that the original idea was hers too. She had planted it using a great deal of subtlety. She had used casual remarks, seemingly given without a thought. She also left books around that had references to spanking or discipline on the back cover blurbs. She even used old movies. Sometimes they watched old films with stars like Elvis or John Wayne that had spanking scenes. She always timed it so that he got there before the spanking scene. They would leave the television on while they talked.

She didn't have to do anything or make any effort to point out the scene, it was enough just to have it on. Her reasons were a secret even to herself.

Now that he had finally responded to her secret plan, she was shocked and puzzled. She wanted to keep her hidden desires secret. She also realized that she was scared and hesitating. Inwardly she wondered why since, unbeknownst to Jerry, this was her idea in the first place. She swallowed hard and met his warm brown eyes.

"Okay." As soon as the word was out she lowered her blue-green eyes shyly and asked, "What exactly do you want me to do?"

"First, I want you to go get a big, wooden spoon from the kitchen. I wouldn't want to hurt my hand." There was that big grin, as cheerful and friendly as ever, with a touch of boyish mischievousness thrown in. "At least, not as much as I'm going to hurt your big, succulent butt."

"Big, my ass!" she muttered as she headed for the kitchen.

"Precisely." She heard him reply in a voice filled with humor. "Big and succulent and very beautiful."

She did as he ordered but she was nervous as hell. She returned with the spoon and stood there shaking slightly, feeling awkward and even somehow exposed with it in her hand.

"Come and stand in front of my chair." He kept his voice soft and gentle, filled with his usual warmth and humor.

Once again she did as he instructed. Moving slowly, almost like she was in a dream, she walked over to stand in front of him. He reached up and gently pulled her forward to stand between his knees. When he reached up and undid the snap and zipper of her jeans, the flutter in the pit of her stomach grew and her knees felt weak.

"Lower your jeans slowly, love," Jerry ordered quietly.

He gently took the wooden spoon from her numb fingers and stuck it into his back pocket.

She lowered her jeans slowly, pushing them all the way down to her ankles and began to step out of them when he stopped her.

"Leave them around your ankles and now bend over my knees. I'm sure you've seen the standard position, it's been in a lot of books and movies," he chided as he gently guided her around to the side of the chair. "Even in some of the movies we've

105

watched together."

In a daze, she did as he instructed, nervously lowering her voluptuous body over his lap. When she was in position he said, "Now I want you to hold off for as long as you can before yelling STOP! You can moan, groan, scream or cry but avoid yelling STOP."

She stayed in position on his lap, her long, dark blonde hair brushing the floor, waiting nervously.

She asked quietly, "Will you stop spanking me when I do yell stop?"

Without answering, he lowered her blue, nylon underwear down to the top of her thighs.

She protested immediately, "Jerry, I've told you time and again, stop trying to pull my pants down!"

It was a long tradition with them. As a part of his attempted seductions he would try to remove her clothes. As a part of her resistance, she protested. It was partially a game and partially in earnest. He always got most of her clothes off, or at least out of the way, and she always managed to stop him short of his real goal, usually by threatening to call 911 as soon as he left.

In truth, Jerry was just one of those men who don't get talked about very often: The men who really understand the meaning of NO. He didn't like the word and he tried to get her to say YES, but he did understand and respect the word.

He ignored her outburst and pushed up the bottom of her dark pink knit top, unsnapped her bra and then began to gently stroke her firm, slightly large, well-rounded butt.

"How else can I spank you bare-bottomed?" he said in a very reasonable tone.

"Then why did you have to unfasten my bra?" she asked with asperity.

"I didn't have to I wanted to because I love your big tits," he laughed.

"And you never answered me when I asked you if you would stop when I ask you to," she snapped at him.

There was a pause before he finally answered her question.

"I'm not sure. Maybe I will or maybe not. Maybe I'll stop just a little bit after you say stop, but then again… "

He played with her checks pulling them apart and rubbing, even pinching them. "Maybe I'll just keep spanking you. I might even spank you a bit harder, you never know. I wonder if I can make your butt the same color as your sweater."

He played with her tight anus with a fingertip. She squirmed and waited, about to panic, about to explode! She was torn between running away and punching his lights out. He put his hand on her butt and rubbed it in a small circle, making the skin feel warm and tingling. All of a sudden his large, work-roughened hand crashed down on that very spot on her left check in a series of sharp, loud slaps. She gasped, then swallowed hard and tried not to cry out. He turned his attention to her right check, first rubbing a circle and then giving it the same harsh treatment.

He stopped spanking her and stroked her butt some more, looking carefully at the first traces of pink, and then he began to spank her once again. He noticed that each slap caused the skin to be white for a split second before the rosy blush appeared. He used slow steady slaps, spanking her much harder than before. Although she continued to keep silent and remained still, she tensed her warm and already burning buttocks.

He stopped at once and said quietly, "Relax your butt."

An aura of unreality came over Ann. She couldn't believe the spanking was happening to her and she couldn't figure out why she wasn't trying to stop it, or at least protesting. Even as she consciously willed herself to try to relax and stop clenching the cheeks of her buttocks together, she wondered in part of her mind why she hadn't yelled stop.

He resumed spanking her. The slaps were coming harder and a little faster. Each one landed with a sharp sound. Her butt began to burn and sting. She began to squirm, the movement causing her to rub up against his zipper and his hard penis. She could feel his erection through his pants. Some of the slaps felt sharper than the rest.

As the spanking continued, at one point she instinctively put her hand back to protect her butt, but he grabbed the hand and rained several fast sharp blows right on the spot she had been trying to shield.

"Never try to protect your butt from me again!" he said sternly.

The pain from those blows was so sharp she cried out, but most of the spanking stung, and she had admitted to herself that in a strange way, it felt really great. It was very painful but also strangely wonderful and exciting. She made up her mind to try to keep from yelling stop for as long as she could. The spanking continued, ever harsher and ever stronger.

Finally when his hand got sore, he started using the spoon. It was much more painful and also colder, much less personal than his hand, but she still tried to be as brave as she could. The stinging spanking continued. Over and over the wooden spoon landed several times on one cheek before moving to the other. The pain grew each time he brought the spoon down.

She finally couldn't hold out any longer. "Stop! God, please stop!"

Instantly Jerry stopped spanking her, then after a long pause when she had begun to relax, he gave her a couple of extra swats on each cheek, very hard, very fast, and finally he was done. He told her to stand with her back to him so he could look at her glowing hot, red butt.

After a few minutes he stood up and walked over behind her. He gently rubbed her tender bottom. He led her over to the sofa and told her to lie down, face down. She obeyed without a word. He gently rubbed some lotion over her hot pink skin. It felt cool, soothing and very sensual.

Finally he asked her to stand up. He pulled up her underwear and jeans and told her to fasten them. He ordered her to sit on the wooden chair. It felt hard against her tender skin but she obeyed.

It was his turn to stand in front of her as she sat in the chair looking down as he spoke to her. "You did great! I never expected you to let me spank you so long and hard, it was fantastic! How did you like it?" he asked with an excited and earnest look on his handsome, olive brown face.

"If I say it was wonderful would you think I was weird?" she laughed, nervously.

"I'd never think you were weird, kinky maybe, but never weird." He gave her that wide, friendly grin of his and leaned over to kiss her gently.

"Then I'll admit I liked it, the stinging, the heat and the feeling of helplessness," she grinned back at him. "I felt like I had given a part of my being over to your use or your abuse. I felt like I trusted you more than I ever trusted anyone else."

"Did it hurt?" he asked curiously.

"Of course, but it was a good hurt, more like a warm, stinging feeling," she answered. "With an occasional sharp, smarting ache thrown in for good luck."

"Well good," he told her, "because you can tell I enjoyed it." He looked down at his pants, his erection tenting out the worn fabric. "God! I'm hard. From now on, whenever and wherever I want to spank you, you will submit, without hesitation and without question. Unless I tell you to struggle." He met her eyes, "And I won't always use my hands or the spoon either. You are going to be responsible for helping me find new things to use on your butt: a hairbrush, a paddle, whatever."

"Remember, I want you to be on the lookout for things that I can use to beat your butt. I want you to look into positions for me to spank you in, things you can lean over that I can spank you on. I also want you to make a set of restraints that I can use to tie you up, and find something I can tie you to, something that will put your butt at just the right height and angle for me to spank you while you're tied and gagged. I also want you to start reading books like *The Pearl* and *The Story of O* so you'll feel like having a spanking when I come over. So you're waiting for me with your butt tingling, filled with anticipation and just a little hint of fear. Lastly, I want you to start writing down our little adventures so we can read them together."

"Does this mean you want me to become more subservient?"

she asked curiously. "I don't think I could."

"Hell, no! I want you as feisty, as hardheaded and as ornery as you are now except for this one thing. Remember, I fell in love with your passion and spirit. I just want this one area of submission. For the rest, please never change."

He took her hand and pulled her out of the chair, leading her to the sofa where they cuddled and sat side by side, quietly talking and halfheartedly watching a movie. He kissed her neck and stroked her hair. He reached under her sweater and fondled her large breasts.

After the movie was over she turned to him.

"Sweetheart?" She looked at him shyly. "My ass has stopped tingling. Would you please spank me again? Harder?"

"Take off your jeans then go find something that I can use as a paddle." Jerry got up and moved back to the chair. He sighed and pretended to act resigned. "It seems like it's true what they say, a man's work is never done."

That was only the first night. They discussed it a few days later and both agreed that they wanted to continue the spankings as long as they were more playful than painful, although sometimes the pain was a part of it.

Like the evening when, in the middle of watching a boring movie on television, Jerry got up and looked casually around Ann's house. He disappeared for a few minutes and returned with something in his hands.

"Can I tie your hands together?" he asked.

"Of course." She trusted him.

He tied her hands together and then, without asking, tied a blindfold over her eyes. He told her to stand up and she did. He pulled down her jeans and ordered her to lay face down on the sofa. She complied, knowing what was coming and still relishing the feelings of helplessness and disorientation caused by the blindfold and the restraint. The spanking wasn't especially long and hard but it was enough to cause her buttocks to get really warm and bright pink. Jerry left the room again and he was gone for a long time. When he returned she felt a cold wet sensation on her butt and heard a shushing sound; he was putting whipped cream on her butt! Jerry sat beside her and licked off the whipped cream, before he untied her and handed her a chocolate sundae.

She finished the sundae. "God, that was good."

"Which? The spanking or the ice cream?"

"Both my love, both."

God, the blank page, starting a new story is hell but some Eveready batteries in the ole vibrator stirred something up, (in my head... boy, are you dirty minded!) I'm lucky that my man is just tough enough, any longer and I'd have to type standing up. I need to get it longer, any suggestions? No, the stories, you perverts, not <u>*That.*</u> *Well,* <u>*That*</u> *too.*

Eight

The Beast: Beauty Over A Log

This is a scene from my forthcoming novel <u>The Heart of the Beast</u>. It's an adult take on <u>Beauty and the Beast</u>. It's not a purely spanking novel but it has several spanking scenes. This is one of the more severe scenes. Later in this book, I've included one of the more humorous spanking scenes.

All in all Beauty was content living with the Beast. Her only real complaints were that once or twice she had gotten a faint glimpse of what real passion and tenderness could be, only to have it snatched away abruptly. She wanted to feel it reach its full depth. She wanted that deeply. She also missed her family and her freedom. Aside from these things and her aching loneliness, Beauty was fairly comfortable.

She was learning to live with her rugged companion without angering him. She was fairly confident that the Beast would never really hurt her. About a week later when she went with the Beast on a short hunting trip, she found out that she was wrong, painfully wrong.

Beauty was thrilled as she waited outside the stables for her mount to be saddled. Not only was she eager to ride again, for it had been years since she had been on a horse, but she was hoping to get a chance to see her brother Tom and mayhap have a quick word with him. The Beast brought her a horse; a gentle but spirited bay mare and helped her to mount. The two men who brought out the horses and dogs were not known to Beauty. Her brother Tom was nowhere to be seen. The Beast was still preventing her from any sight or word with her family. Beauty swallowed her disappointment and gloried in the feel of a horse

112

beneath her, the crispness of the fall breeze, and the chance to spend a whole day racing through the woods. They were off!

Although she didn't get to see her brother, Beauty was still excited to be out riding with the Beast. It was the first time the Beast had ever taken her with him anywhere, even hunting. Beauty did not enjoy the hunting itself. She had never come to enjoy the sight of animals being chased down and slaughtered. She reveled in the beauty of the countryside and the feel of a horse beneath her, even though she knew that she would be sore from the hours of unaccustomed riding.

The Beast and a few of his soldiers were replenishing the castle's supplies of meat. They released the dogs to run down the wild boars. They used short stout lances, easier to work with in the thick forest than their regular lances, to kill whatever boars the dogs ran down. They dressed down the day's catch in the forest, salting some of the meat, drying some and cooking the rest.

The Beast was angered by the signs of poachers he found in the forest. Standing over the carcass of a slaughtered deer, his temper raged.

"I'm going to find these poachers and hang them!" he bellowed. "That will teach the scum that poaching in these woods is the same as stealing from me."

"It makes me wonder, M'lord," Beauty said thoughtfully, eyeing the spoiled remains with distaste, "why would any of the villagers be willing to run the risk of poaching? How desperate must they be to be willing to face your wrath?"

"Do you seek to excuse them for poaching?" the Beast yelled at her. "Or do you attempt to persuade me to show them mercy for the crime?"

"Neither M'lord, I but wondered what led them to take such a risk." Beauty met his eyes openly. "They must know what penalty you would put on the killing of your game."

The Beast turned away from Beauty without answering her but he pondered her remarks for a long time. He knew full well that the villagers feared and even hated him. Her questions ate at him. Why would they take such a risk? The thought came to him of what risks he would be willing to take if it were his family that was starving. He said no more about it but the thought remained in his mind for several days.

The next day disaster struck! As the small band of hunters was fording a swift but shallow river, one of the younger guards lost control of his horse and was thrown. The guard probably could have stood up in the shallow water, but between his terror and the weight of his clothes, boots and sword, he could not get a purchase with his feet. He thrashed about in the water, panicked and unable to swim. The Beast leaped off his horse to rescue the lad and handed his heavy sword to the nearest person. It just happened to be Beauty.

Beauty's horse was also spooked, panicked by the guard's horse bumping into her and the shouting of the men. She struggled to keep her mount under control but her horse slipped on a wet rock and almost went down. As she wrestled to remain seated and to help her horse regain his footing, the sword slipped from her grasp. She gave a startled cry as she saw it fall over a small waterfall and squarely into the one deep pool in the river.

The Beast was soaked and irritated as he carried the unconscious young guard to the shore. He struggled to revive the man but his efforts were to no avail. The Beast turned away, coldly ordering the other guards to bury the body. He was exceedingly angry and frustrated. His clothes were stuck to his body and his best leather boots were probably ruined. That was when he realized that Beauty had dropped his sword. It was the final straw. That was also when she found out that the Beast could and would indeed hurt her.

She discovered it the hard way, bending over a hollow log in the forest, naked from the waist down with the Beast using his thick leather belt on her buttocks and legs without the least hint of mercy. It was the first time he'd ever hit her with anything but the palm of his hand and it hurt greatly.

He ignored her screams as he lashed at her red ass repeatedly, each swing of his strong arm causing a welt or a bruise. The whole of her bottom was covered with painful red stripes and purplish blotches.

Worst of all for Beauty, the Beast's guards were well within earshot and even as she writhed in pain she knew they heard and enjoyed every swish and crack of the belt, every sob and every scream.

Finally the Beast stopped and coldly ordered, "Stand up."

He put his belt back on. It was over. The voice he commanded her with brooked no denial or disobedience. Beauty tried to comply but she was too stiff and sore, and much too shaken to her core. Her legs failed her and she sank to the ground, weeping openly.

"Cease that at once, woman!" he commanded, but without any real anger behind the words.

The Beast started to reach down to her then hesitated and sat stiffly on the hollow log. He pulled her onto his lap, ignoring her sore bottom as he cuddled her gently. She clung to him as she continued to cry. Her sobs seemed to last forever but when her tears finally began to ease the Beast quickly shifted her position until she was face down over his knees.

Beauty panicked and struggled to right herself but to no avail. Holding her in place with one iron hand he stroked her hot, flaming ass, gently touching the welts. He explored her moist femininity with his fingers before he withdrew his hand to spank her with lightly stinging, almost gentle spanks.

For long moments he held her like that, alternately stroking her hot bottom, fingering her moist core and almost gently spanking her. Finally, he used his hands to bring her to the heights of ecstasy.

After she came he held her shivering body until the shutters stopped, then he coldly pushed her off his knees and ordered her to stand up and straighten her dress. Although she was shaking with both pleasure and pain, this time she did as he ordered without any further delay.

When she finally walked stiffly behind the Beast as he led her back to the camp, the men were staring at her and laughing.

115

Crude remarks floated towards her on the cool night air. The Beast suddenly picked her up and carried her over to a small tent set a small pace apart from the men. He threw her face down onto a soft pallet of furs. He grasped her hips in his hands and pulled her roughly to her knees. Without any preliminaries or finesse he entered her, sodomizing her even as she cried anew. She gasped and even screamed several times at the unfamiliar pain.

She was still sobbing as he rolled away. "That hurt!"

"It's just the first time, like the other virginity," the Beast murmured. "It gets easier with time."

"M'lord?" Beauty asked gently, "Why haven't you done it that way before?"

"I prefer the usual way," the Beast replied. "I usually only do it that way if the woman wants to prevent a pregnancy."

"Then why tonight?" Beauty asked curiously.

"Because I was irritated with you and I felt like it," the Beast told her sternly.

"I'm sorry, M'lord," she sobbed, her hands gently grasping her own butt. "Truly, I didn't mean to displease you."

"Displease me?" The Beast was once again furious. "You dropped my favourite sword into the deepest part of the river and you think I'm displeased? I'm far past displeased and if you don't know it then maybe I better take you back to the log and add to your welts."

"If that's your wish M'lord, I await your pleasure." Beauty said softly, still crying. "But I truly am sorry. I'll swim out to get it tomorrow."

"You can swim?" The Beast felt his anger fade.

He was amazed because none of his men could swim. He was a poor swimmer himself, as the day's disaster proved.

"Yes M'lord," Beauty sighed wearily, ignoring his surprise. "Shall I prepare myself for another whipping?"

"Nay Lass," the Beast told her softly. "I think I have another use for you tonight."

To her amazement he got a moist cloth, as he had on their first

116

night together and washed her, soothing her tender parts. After he finished the task he proceeded to spend an eternity loving her slowly and thoroughly with his hands and mouth, even turning her over to gently kiss her welts. He lightly nipped her round firm buttocks, then licked the injured spot. Finally he turned her onto her back and lowered his mouth to her soft tangle of moist curls. It was a long time before he entered her, and for once he moved slowly, almost leisurely inside her before picking up the pace. In spite of her welts and tenderness, for the first time she felt the full measure of a climax with him as they reached the peak together. One of the young foot soldiers sleeping nearby heard her scream her release as she reached her climax.

"God's blood!" the young man exclaimed. "Isn't he ever going to cease beating the poor girl?"

An older guardsman sleeping nearby laughed openly, "Lad, we need to find you a woman and quickly!"

"Did I whip you too hard?" the Beast asked as he held her gently before they slept. "I was angry and so frustrated by the death of the guard that I may have overreacted a bit."

"It's not my place to say, M'lord. Indeed, I am at your disposal," Beauty replied calmly, but inside her heart leaped as she realized that for the first time ever the Beast had almost admitted he was wrong and had even come close to an apology. "Do with me as you please."

"And if I decided to kill you or turn you over to one of my men for a plaything?" the Beast asked.

"It's your decision, M'lord." Beauty kept her eyes downcast, hiding her quick spark of temper from him. "I have no say in the matter."

"How about a kiss instead?" the Beast whispered gruffly, bending down to her.

"If that is your wish, M'lord," she smiled at him, a wide dazzling smile. "I but seek to obey you and please you."

The Beast stopped before kissing her, his mouth almost touching her soft lips as he whispered softly, "I just love meekness in a woman, Beauty. It's too bad your meekness is a sham. Did you think I was fooled?"

She reached up a slender arm and stroked his long, silky hair. "You're no fool, M'lord, and I'd fight anyone who dared say so."

The Beast laughed softly as he kissed her. Beauty met his kiss willingly, responding with a passion of her own. It was still rare that he kissed her, then she pulled him down on top of her, ignoring the ache in her bottom as she sank back onto the soft bed of furs. He didn't press her back into the furs and enter her; however to her amazement, he lowered his mouth to her breasts, nibbling them before he traced a line of kisses down her soft belly to the thatch or curls guarding her femininity.

For the only time since their first night together, he brought her to the heights of ecstasy with an intimate kiss that seemed to fill her very soul with sensuous joy.

This time the young soldier merely pulled a blanket over his head and ignored her cries.

The Beast reached for her as her shivers ceased but she said softly, "Not this time, my fine lord."

She pushed him gently onto his back and he went willingly. He let her do what she wanted. He could scarcely believe the depth of his emotion, his joy and his pride, as she returned his intimate kiss. Although she did whatever he asked, it was the first time she had ever initiated such an action. He soon found out what difference there was between compliance and enthusiastic participation. Before they slept, they made love again. This time she rode astride him, completely wanton in her passion.

The next morning they sent most of the guards back to the castle, keeping only two men with them. The two guards, experienced hunters, were stalking deer with their bows. The Beast had been craving fresh venison for his table. This day Beauty and the Beast did not hunt; instead they tarried by the river, resting and talking softly. The Beast, for once, asked her opinion on several minor matters before he came to the one thing that had preyed upon his mind.

"Beauty, if you were me, what would you do about the poachers?" the Beast asked, lying beside her on the riverbank.

"I know not, M'lord, for 'tis not an easy problem. The serfs have to have enough to eat but your game should be protected," Beauty smiled as she stroked back a lock of hair from his face. "Not just for your use, but to ensure that game will always be plentiful in these woods. Some of the serfs, not all, but some are so lazy that they would rather poach than toil on their farms, while some others are truly starving. I think they deserve different punishments even though the crime is the same."

"But there should be some punishments?" the Beast asked pointedly.

"Yes," Beauty admitted against her will, "but the villagers should have some protection against starving and their awful poverty too."

"I'll think about it." The Beast reluctantly stood up and pulled Beauty to her feet, "We had best return to the castle, these woods are not safe without a guard nearby."

Back at the stables the Beast helped Beauty dismount, overlooking the presence of her brother Tom. She was thrilled to see her brother but afraid to let her emotions show. Not by word or gesture did she acknowledge his proximity or their relationship. The Beast ignored Tom too. In fact, he talked to Beauty about the poachers' right in front of her brother.

Handing the reins of his charger to Tom, he said, "I think I'll start sending a small group of guards out to patrol the woods for poachers. Not with Gerrin, but mayhap I'll put Gregory in charge. He needs more experience. I'll tell him to go out every third day and order that he should bring all the poachers he catches back to me, still alive, to await my judgment."

As they walked back to the castle Beauty whispered to the Beast, "M'lord, if you truly want to catch the poachers, you should not have let Tom hear the schedule for your patrols. He can warn the villagers. And, why did you put Gregory in charge when Gerrin is so much more experienced and ruthless?"

"Because, my dear Beauty, Gerrin really is so much more ferocious," the Beast grinned, "and I hope Tom does warn the villagers. Why do you think I said it in front of him? I'm not a fool."

He whistled as he strode into the castle, leaving Beauty staring after him with her mouth agape.

The Beast is a temperamental and devious man, hard-hearted and hard to please. I wonder if he will be tamed by Beauty's patience and passion? It's a fairy tale so I expect they will live happily ever after. The real question is does happily ever after include spankings? For me, it does.

Nine

Kiss My *What?*

Who hasn't wondered at one time or another if two actors playing loves scenes could lead to something more, something real and lasting. Oh, I know that every time one of them is interviewed about a sexy movie scene they claim it's just work, not really fun and romantic. Okay, I can believe it. In the hottest scenes they have people all over the place, directors giving orders, lighting angles, dialogue and cues to remember. But then how many times have we heard about two people making a movie, and suddenly they divorce their respective spouses and move in together? Even marry each other? What then might happen if two single actors meet doing local theater? Could a love scene lead to something more? Could a spanking scene lead to true romance? Why not?

Clay woke up earlier than his wife, Sherry. He didn't wake her; he just lay there next to her and thought about their lives together and how they had met. It wasn't that long ago, only a few years. It was hard to even remember his life before Sherry.

They were inseparable now, married, and new parents. They were also kinky. They were both active members of *The Paddle Club*, as were most of their friends. He smiled to himself in the growing light of the new day. He couldn't believe how far they had come since the day they first met.

They had been Paddle Club members for over three years and lovers for five. They had been put together by an unintentional matchmaker, the director of a musical play for the community theater.

That's how they met: When they both auditioned for parts in a musical that the Community Theater was putting on. As it happened, Clay got the male lead and Sherry the female lead. The musical was *Kiss Me Kate*, based very loosely on William Shakespeare's *The Taming of the Shrew*.

Neither one had much acting experience, but both of them had good voices and had received some training. Sherry was a natural soprano who had taken voice lessons for a time. Clay had a strong, romantic tenor. He had been in his Church choir, and back in the day, in school choruses throughout his education.

They were both doing well in the play since it called for overacting and dramatic speeches, not realism. They worked well together and felt an instant attraction and chemistry that gave an added push to their acting.

They had one problem though, one scene that never seemed to come out right: the spanking scene. It just never seemed comical, melodramatic or even realistic. It just seemed dull and flat.

The director asked them to get together after practice and work on the scene by themselves. He suggested they try to "liven it up" and even "build up some sexual tension" between the two of them. They had sexual tension even if the director didn't know it, so that wasn't the problem. The problem was with that one scene, and it had to do with spanking.

The director had really missed something, big time! They had the chemistry and the sexual tension, but were both suppressing it for various reasons. She was shy. He was harried at work and busy with the play. He planned on keeping in touch with her after the play when he had more time to get to know her as a person, not Kate the shrew.

Following the director's suggestion they stayed late at the theater to rehearse the scene a few times, but with no real results, they ended up going out to dinner together. The dinner was filled with unspoken longings and romance but as far as the scene? It didn't help. Not at all.

Finally Clayton had an outlandish idea. He asked Sherry to come over to his house for dinner and a private rehearsal. He also told her to wear the full skirts she wore to rehearse in. He had a plan that he was quite sure Sherry would not like. In fact, he had a little surprise in store for her. He knew she'd get mad, he just hoped she wouldn't get too mad. He really wanted to keep in touch with her after the show ended. Who was he kidding? He thought he wanted her in his bed for a long time, maybe forever. She was perfect for him. She was a nice girl, but that seemed far too tame a description for her. She was fun and funny, intelligent, sweet, caring and quirky. And of course, she was one of the most beautiful women he'd ever seen.

Clayton set up a video camera and they worked on the scene. The first time through they did it the same way they had always done it, but they tried to put more feeling into it. Afterwards they sat and watched the tape of their practice.

Watching it, Sherry sounding thoroughly disgusted said, "It just doesn't work, even for a amateur theater. It lacks something. It's dull."

"Let's try it again, I have an idea," Clay said with a grin. "It may help."

They did the scene again, only this time he didn't give her a fake spanking over her thick, lacy petticoats. Instead, he flipped the petticoats up onto her back and pulled down her underwear. Then he gave her a very real, very hard and very painful spanking right on her bare butt! She squealed and squirmed as his hand descended in loud slaps, punctuating her futile struggles.

Sherry was shocked. She had never even dreamed of being spanked as an adult by a man. Let alone a man she dreamed about, a man she wanted to get to know more intimately. She was glad she found out what a brute Clayton was before she got too involved with him. She struggled and yelled out loud. When he let her up she slapped Clayton hard, right across the mouth. He ignored the slap and cuddled her gently, speaking softly to her and calming her down.

Finally when she was calmed down they watched the videotape together. They both had to admit it: The performance was better; it had the real quality the director wanted. Clay told her so.

"That's because it *was* real, dolt," Sherry steamed at him. "I don't care how good it is," she told him firmly, "there is no way you're going to give me such a hard spanking, and for sure no way you're going to get me to go bare butt on stage."

"But it is better if I really spank you, isn't it?" Clay asked reasonably in that quiet manner of his.

"Yes, I guess," Sherry admitted, mumbling. "But does it have to be so hard?"

"Well, was it really too painful?" he asked, probing. "Or were you just surprised?"

"Yes, it was painful. But of course it was more of a shock than anything," she admitted. "There was some real pain but it faded quickly."

"Could you take it? On stage, I mean?" he pushed. "Without going bare bottom, of course."

"Sure, for eight performances, I guess I could," she admitted weakly.

"Then get a pair of lacy pantaloons and I can spank you over them," Clayton grinned. "I won't spank you as hard or the same way each time, so there will still be some surprise and some freshness in each performance. How does that sound?"

"Like *you* should play Kate." She raised her eyebrows at him.

"Sorry, but I don't fit in the costume," he grinned at her. "Even if I did, you look much better in it than I do."

"I think we should leave the slap in," she teased.

"Surprise me." He winked at her.

He stood up and walked her to the door. He stopped at the door enfolding her in a warm hug, and kissed her for the first time ever, except on stage. The kiss quickly grew. After that first kiss she didn't go home. They went straight to his bedroom and made love all night long. He was exhausted at work the next day but it was well worth it. By the time the play opened she had moved in with him and they were both ecstatic together. The passion was real and intense but the quiet times between the passion, the everyday moments, were wonderful too. They fit, they blended, and complemented each other.

The play was a great success. Clayton spanked Sherry nightly on stage, usually not extremely hard but for opening night he was relentless. On closing night, Sherry had a surprise for him.

In spite of her nervousness, on closing night she left off her lacy pantaloons. Clay didn't find out until he flipped up her petticoats in the scene. In spite of the surprise he gave her a very hard spanking right there on stage, directly on her bare butt! It was a miracle they didn't get arrested. Their only saving grace was the voluminous petticoats that hid her nudity. Some of the audience members thought there was something... but no, down to the last person, they decided they must be insane. They wouldn't, would they?

Neither one of them ever really admitted even to themselves what was going on, until they caught themselves practicing the spanking scene one night about a month after the run of the musical had ended. They gave up acting and joined *The Paddle Club*.

This is a just quick scene from my novel The Paddle Club, *just a small taste. The novel has spanking ranging from fun and playful to discipline, with both men and women topping and bottoming. I mainly put it in because the movie was on as I was compiling this book.*

If you've never seen the movie Kiss Me Kate, *you should. The voices are splendid. The dancing is great. And the spanking scene is... well, the word that comes to mind is lusty. A longer, harder spanking than is shown in most mainstream movies, but not bare bottom, of course. Still a worthy movie spank scene, and often overlooked.*

Ten

The Spanking Of The Shrew

What happens if the bitch deserves it? What if she fights back? How far can a man, even a gentle man, be pushed? Is this a self-portrait? Heavens! I hope not!

The big blow-up happened when Sue and Mike had just been living together for about six weeks. Before that time they were generally a very happy couple. They were very close and supportive of each other. They shared similar outlooks, both fairly conservative, and had compatible interests and viewpoints. Sue loved dogs and Mike loved horses, but they were both animal lovers. They were tender and loving to each other out of bed, and uninhibited and passionate in bed. Both of them liked to have sex frequently and neither had any inhibitions with the other.

They just seemed to fit together perfectly in most ways, even in their appearance. They both had red hair, although hers was lighter, flaming, and his was more auburn. They both had bright green eyes. He was tall, 6'3" and muscular. She was medium height, 5' 4" and well-rounded, almost plump. He had bulging biceps and she had full, thrusting breasts and a well-rounded bottom.

There was one small fly in the ointment though. One small area in which Sue and Mike had completely different personalities: They had completely different temperaments. Sue was moody; she could either be funny and very loving, or irritable. Irritable was almost too mild a word for it; the truth was, when the dark mood came over her Sue could be a flat out bitch from hell. It didn't happen very often, but when her

126

temper erupted most people ran and hid if they had any common sense at all.

Mike's personality was much more level. He was easygoing and patient. He never seemed to be in a bad mood, never lost his patience or his sense of fun. In a way, that fueled Sue's dark temper even more.

They both cared for each other very deeply and their different tempers seemed to be a small problem, easy to overlook. Sometimes it even seemed to add spice to their relationship. Her wildness was even out done by his calm, good-humored disposition. Most of the time he could turn her bad moods into passion; in fact, some of the wildest sex they ever had was when he had to romance her out of one of her black moods, or even when he just let her have her temper tantrum. When it was over, he would take her to bed and they would have a sexual marathon that ended only when neither one of them could move.

The sexual release made her bad moods bearable, and they thought they had the problem under control. One thing they both forgot though was that even good humor and passion can only go so far.

The storm hit during one of the worst bitchy periods of Sue's life; even she knew it, but she couldn't seem to get control of herself. She was nagging and picking at Mike all day long. She heard herself bitching at Mike and wondered to herself why she couldn't just shut the hell up.

Finally Mike was totally exasperated and asked her as calmly as possible, "Why are you being such a bitch today? What can I do to get you to relax, or at least to shut up and leave me alone?"

"I don't know what's bugging me," she admitted slowly. "Everything's messed up at work. I'm not doing well in my class over at the college. I'm terrified. I'm afraid I'm losing you. I feel like I can't do anything right. I hate myself when I'm like this." She paced the room stopping to look at him. "I know that I'm being terrible but I can't help it; the more I try to bring myself under control, the louder and nastier I get. I'm out of control. I feel like I want to smash somebody in the face or just sit here and cry. But smashing somebody in the face sounds much better, definitely my first choice." She took a deep breath and shook back her long red hair. "And I don't think there's anything you can do about it, not one damn thing."

"Nothing?" he asked gently, really concerned to see her so upset.

She snapped suddenly, sparks in her big green eyes, "No! Nothing! If you don't want to be near me, just go the hell away! Just take all that phony concern and get the hell out of my face! There's not a goddamn thing you can say or do that will improve my mood, so just go away and do whatever you want!"

That was it, she had gone too far!

"If you don't really care what I do, I might as well do what I really want to. What I really want to do at this very minute is to give you a spanking that you'll never forget!" It was the first time he had ever shown her that he even had a temper.

He reached for her, intending to reinforce the threat that had only been meant to shake her up. At least that's all he intended until she socked him in the jaw!

The fight that followed was one sided because only one side was really trying to hurt the other. The other side was acting strictly on the defense. He was taller and more muscular, definitely much stronger, but she was really trying to inflict bodily harm. All he was trying to do was subdue her and avoid being injured!

He was too surprised from the punch in the jaw to react as fast as he should have, so she managed a quick kick to his shin as a follow up. He made a grab for her and came away with a ripped piece of her silk blouse, which only made her more irate. It was her favorite blouse! She ignored the shreds of fabric hanging from her arms and tried to scratch his face, snarling like a wounded possum.

He tried reason. "Sue! Stop fighting! Let's sit down and talk."

"You say that you want to give me a spanking I'll never forget and then say let's talk!" she shrieked. "About what? Pain? Bruises? Are you nuts?"

A small vase sailed past his head, narrowly missing him and crashing against the wall. Shards of broken glass and flowers scattered on the floor while water ran down the wall dripping into a small puddle on the floor. Both Sue and Mike ignored the dripping mess.

"I didn't mean it, sweetheart, I was just trying to shake you up and make you see how crazy you were acting. Come on, relax." He still tried against all odds to keep his temper in check.

The vase was followed by a book, a large hardcover book. He ducked and tried to get her in a bear hug but failed when he had to dodge the knee aimed with deadly force at his crotch. That did it! Finally, he was really mad; not just annoyed, not just exasperated, but flat out furious in a way that any man is when threatened with sudden, painful emasculation. The promised spanking was not just a threat, it was soon going to be a reality, even if it killed him! He ducked his head and darted into the bedroom.

"Chicken!" she yelled after him, and threw a shoe.

He came out of the bedroom hiding something in one hand, and had something else stuffed into his pocket. He got as close as he dared to get to her, then reached out and caught her hand when she tried to slap his face. He used the pantyhose that he had hidden in his hand to wrap around her wrist. She tried to kick him again, then struggled wildly as he managed to get the hose looped around her other wrist. He tied the ends of the hose together, tightly.

He pulled a second pair of pantyhose from his pocket, then ducked and looped that pair around her knees. When he tightened the loop around her legs, she lost her balance and fell with a loud thud onto the hardwood floor. Quickly, he tied a knot into the loop around her knees.

Picking her up and throwing her over his shoulder, he slapped her sharply on the butt before he carried her into the bedroom and tossed her onto the bed. He got a third pair of pantyhose from her drawer and tied her hands to the bed's headboard. She was laying face down. She squirmed and struggled and finally managed to turn over.

"Let me up, you bastard!" she yelled, fear and fury mixed in her voice.

"I'll do whatever I want, whenever I want, you've had your way long enough!" He was so mad he could hardly see straight. "When you started to fight me, all I really wanted to do was comfort you. Now I fully intend to give you that spanking I mentioned! And I mean for it to hurt like hell!"

He stormed out of the room, not returning for at least fifteen minutes.

"Have you calmed down yet?" he asked. The short break had given him time to regain his temper and he was trying to give her every chance to make up with him.

"Mike, please let me up, these knots are hurting me. Please." She sounded much better, a lot calmer.

Mike didn't quite trust her, despite her attempt to appear cool and collected. He decided to give her one last chance before making the final judgment, to spank or not to spank. To test her out he untied her legs. He spent a few seconds rubbing each leg where the pantyhose had been wrapped around it. Unbeknownst to her, he was being very wary, and rightfully so as it turned out. In spite of his caution she kicked him with her foot, actually catching him in the nose as he sat on the bed and rubbed her feet. Blood spurted out, getting on the sheets and on both of them. The final judgment was made; she was definitely going to get the promised spanking. It was going to be a very hard spanking too.

Mike left the bedroom. Sue was still tied around the knees and lying on her back, with her hands still tied to the brass bed. Mike was on a quest in search of a strap or another suitable weapon. He wanted to give her a long, hard spanking and he sure wasn't going to hurt his hand as badly as he was going to hurt her butt!

He looked at several things but none of them seemed right. He wanted something that would hurt her and sting like hell, but without raising welts. With the way she was acting, the bitch would go to the cops!

He settled on something so obvious that it practically jumped up at him: a small cutting board shaped like a paddle. It was solid wood and almost a half-inch thick. He slapped it against one palm. It made a loud smack and stung where it landed, and that was just one little smack! On her bare buttocks it should sting and burn like hell, especially if he put some force into the blows. With his choice of weapon firmly in hand, he went into the bedroom.

"Roll over, smart-ass, and get your bottom up in the air!" he commanded firmly.

"Hell no, you son of a bitch!" Enraged, she practically spat the words at him.

"Then I'll use this paddle on your breasts!" He sounded like he meant it.

She searched his face and saw that he was implacable. After a long moment her better judgment finally won the day and she rolled over, slowly and reluctantly. He had a pair of scissors in his hand which he used to cut a snip into her skirt, then he grabbed the material in his hands and ripped it up the back. He cut off her underwear, and all the while she kept cussing him out. She started to roll over again.

"Your choice, bitch, your breasts or your ass," he said in a commanding and implacable voice.

She lay back down on her stomach. With her head resting on her hands and a small corner of the pillow stuffed into her mouth, he pulled the rest of the material from her ruined clothes out of the way. She was determined not to give him the satisfaction of making her yell out or cry.

"Get up on your knees. Stick that big ass of yours up in the air," he ordered, more to humiliate her than for any other reason.

"I may not be able to stop you from using that on me," she protested, "but I'm sure as hell not going to put myself in a submissive position for it. I'm not going to make this any easier for you in any way, you asshole. And my butt's not that big! Jerk!"

He went and got a heavy leather western style belt from the

closet. "Which would you rather have me use to beat you?"

He swung the belt and hit her as hard as he could with it causing her to scream, then he swatted her sharply with the paddle.

"Thank God this apartment is well soundproofed. It's up to you: lay there and I'll use the belt, or stick that big but beautiful butt up and I'll just use the paddle." He offered her the grim choice.

Reluctantly she put herself in the requested position, on her knees, with her forearms and head down and her bottom stuck well up in the air. He gently tapped her bottom once with the cutting board then raised it and brought it down with a resounding crack, and the beating began. He paddled her with hard, slow strokes, each one sounding like a shot as it landed on her ass. CRACK! Moving from side to side, he covered the entire area of her buttocks. CRACK! CRACK! He even moved down to the tops of her thighs.

She gave a muffled gasp at each swat. CRACK! The impact of the paddle caused the flesh of her soft bottom to jiggle slightly, and the skin to take on a bright rosy hue, with some darker splotches mixed in.

After about three dozen, a dozen on each cheek and the ones on her thighs, Mike stopped and looked at her butt. It was bright red and hot to the touch, blotchy but it showed no signs of real bruising. He stopped spanking her and walked away, leaving her tied up. She was gasping but not even crying yet.

"Untie me you stupid jerk, you've had your fun," she yelled at him as he left the room.

"You thought that was fun?" He shook his head.

"Please!" she shouted.

Ignoring her, he went into the kitchen and got an ice pack. Seeing it, she thought for a minute it was for her sore, hot butt, until he used it on his own bloody nose.

"Let me up! Bastard!" The sight of him holding that ice pack to his nose was the final straw. She was tired of being tied up and her bottom was sore!

"But sweetheart," he said gently, in a calm reasonable tone, "I haven't finished my job. I'm not done beating your butt." He sounded like he thought she should realize that fact. "I promised to give you a spanking you would always remember. Well, I haven't really begun. We're certainly not nearly there yet."

He leaned down to plant a soft kiss on each cheek of her red-hot ass then he went into the living room and sat down and watched the football game until half time.

As the half-time reports began he sighed dramatically and got up, returning to the bedroom. "I guess it's time for part two. A man's work is never done. You know the drill, get that butt up."

This time she raised herself into position on her knees without a word of protest. He began to punish her again, harder and harder, faster too. Covering the same area as he had before, he paddled her butt again. This time he gave her two dozen solid smacks on each side; a full dozen on each thigh. She gasped each time the paddle landed on her soft, red bottom. The last four blows on each cheek were explosive, very much harder still. CRACK! CRACK! The gasps became high-pitched yelps. CRACK! CRACK!

Once again, he rested. He sat beside her on the bed and gently ran his hand over her red, hot butt; bruises were beginning to show. This is going well, he thought, it won't take too much longer to break her. He had to spank her to a point of submission or else she would have won. Instinctively he knew that if she won, she would be even more vicious than before. She would make his life a living hell. He gave her a full half-hour to rest and to worry before he entered the bedroom again.

"Ready, red butt?" he asked her in a pleasant, conversational tone. "Let's see, first I gave you one dozen on each side, then two. I guess now it should be three dozen. Does that sound all right to you?"

She began to curse again but stopped when he looped a scarf around her throat and got it in position in front of her mouth.

"Open up." She refused. "Come on, dearie, or I'll use my belt on your ass."

She obeyed and he tied the gag. It was a blessed relief. With the crook of one finger he gestured for her to get into position, and gave her the three dozen on each cheek. They were harder still and spaced out so that each crack of the paddle was a separate torture, prolonging the agony. She was sobbing, almost choking, behind the gag. Finally, he had her crying.

He said to her in a quite pleasant manner, "I hope you don't mind but I think we'll wait until the football game is over before we go for four dozen on each cheek. I want the pain from this little session to have plenty of time to sink in before I paddle you any more."

He had just sat down to watch the second half of the game when the doorbell rang. He walked into the bedroom before he answered it.

"If you make a sound or if you do anything to cause whoever that is to be suspicious, there will be a payback that you will never forget," he warned her. "I'll make this little session seem like a child's playtime."

He answered the door. The visitor turned out to be Ernie, the next door neighbor.

"Hey Mike, are you watching the game?" Ernie asked, entering. "My TV set's out."

"Come on in, Ernie," Mike grinned. "I see you brought some beer."

"I figured if you supplied the TV, I could bring the beer," Ernie grinned. "Where's Sue?"

"She can't watch the game with us," Mike told him seriously. "She's tied up today."

"Bummer." The expression made middle-aged Ernie sound like a surfer.

The two men watched as their favorite team trounced the visitors. When the game was over, Mike made his excuses to get rid of Ernie.

"I'd ask you to stay, Ernie, but I have to help Sue with something," he said with a smile. "And you know she'll make my life hell if I don't do it."

"That's okay, Mike," Ernie said man to man. "If I leave her hanging, Maude tears a piece off my hide, let me tell you."

Mike let Ernie out, then, true to his word, he went back into the bedroom, the paddle once again in his hand. She was still crying.

He took off her gag and asked her very nicely, "Well hot cheeks, are you ready for four dozen on each side?"

Without a word, she raised herself to her knees and stuck her butt up in the air. He picked up the paddle and brought it down as hard as he possibly could on her flaming red, hot ass. CRACK! Finally she lost it. She began to sob and tried to say something, fighting hard to get the words out between her sobs: "Please... Please... Sorry... N... No more... Sorry... Please... Sorry... Bitch... Deserved... Please... Sorry... " she sobbed, struggling to get out the words.

He brought the paddle down on her other cheek just as hard. He gave her three more harsh stinging blows on each cheek.

"To finish it off," he said quietly, then left the room.

In a short while, she called him, still sobbing. "Mike, can I get up? I have to go to the bathroom!"

"So wait, and if you wet the bed, I'll repeat the whole damn thing." The nice guy was completely gone and there was no trace of sympathy in his icy, commanding voice.

In a little while he looked in on her and saw that she had, luckily, aside from the lone long welt caused by the blow from the belt, only a few bruises and some red splotches that were already fading. He untied her and she ran for the bathroom. As soon as she closed the bathroom door he placed a chair under the doorknob, locking her inside. He left her there for two hours. When he finally opened the door, he had picked up all signs of her ruined clothes and the debris and broken glass from their fight.

He was sitting on the bed when she emerged. He looked at her and said calmly, "Get dressed and get packed. Get out of my house. Get out of my life!'

"GOD! Mike no! I love you!" she sobbed as she dropped to

the floor in a heap. "Please don't throw me out."

"Then you have to change your ways. Do whatever it takes, go to a shrink, or a witch doctor, or your priest, or whatever else. But you must change your ways." He was firm, leaving no doubt that he meant exactly what he said.

She looked at him with a shy smile, tears streaming down her cheeks. "Can't I just come straight out and ask you to spank me the next time?"

"It would be better than breaking my nose or trying to kick me in the family jewels," he gave her a rueful grin. "We might want to make love again someday. Right now it seems doubtful to me but anything's possible."

"I wouldn't want to disable your handy gadget, I do have a use for it real soon." She looked at him, "I have a question. Please remember that it's purely hypothetical and not a threat. What if I go to the cops?"

"Look in the mirror. I didn't bruise you very much and you're hardly even red. With a paddle, as I know very well from when I was a kid, it takes a lot to bruise. You're just barely red and you're hot, however your butt will cool down soon. Besides, do you really want to show the, um, shall we call it the evidence to the cops?"

"No." She took his hand and kissed it. "I just want to go to bed; like you just said I'm hot, not just on my butt, all over."

"I'm not sure I ever want to touch you again and now you're horny, great." He was rigidly sarcastic.

"Are you sure you never want to touch me again?" she asked slyly, looking down at his erection. "Or did you get turned on by paddling my ass? Could it be that you're just a little ashamed by your body's obvious reaction to your macho display of primitive male violence?"

"Could it be that you enjoyed the pain? Are you a masochist?" he returned.

"I hated the pain but for some reason, I felt like I needed it. I needed to be mastered. I needed to be punished. I know that I pushed you into it, and I don't understand why I did it." She drew a deep breath. "I only know that I love you and I want you right now. I'm horny as hell."

He walked up to stand right in front of her and reached around her grabbing her buttocks roughly in both hands, squeezing them almost savagely. He kissed her deeply and looked into her eyes.

"I love you and I was afraid I was going to lose you. I still say you need counseling, and we need it together," Mike explained. "Not because you like to be spanked once in a while, but because the way you went about expressing that desire pushed me past a little spanking into real violence. The kind of violence that could either escalate or break us up. I didn't know I had that kind of violence in me, and I'm shocked." He kissed her again and lifted her into his arms, backing her up against the wall and somehow managing to unzip his pants before entering her.

He fucked her standing there, her head slamming into the wall with the force of his thrusts and his big strong hands tightly grasping her throbbing buttocks. Finally he staggered over and dropped her on the bed.

Mike stripped off his clothes and joined her quickly. He slid into her again without any preliminaries and they made love with a passion and intensity that shocked them both. Mike was usually a passionate yet tender lover, but this time he was forceful, thrusting into her velvet warmth over and over. He was fully conscious of the pain his hard thrusts must be causing on her hot, tender ass, but the thought only excited him even more.

Sue felt the pain from the spanking and for her it was also an added excitement, an extra sensation. They climbed steadily towards the peak and eased off at the last moment, time and time again. When they both agreed without any thought or coherent words to crest the peak, they were left gasping and shaking with the force of their perfect shared orgasms. They laid there breathing heavily and wet with sweat.

Sue finally spoke about the demons that were driving her. "Mike I know I've always been moody and temperamental, but lately there's something else, something bothering me that I don't quite understand. I'm not trying to hide anything from you but everything has been happening so fast and been so ugly and indefinite that I'm scared. The thing is, I'm not sure what it is that I'm scared of." She kissed him deeply. "The one thing I'm sure of is that my problem isn't you. I really love you."

"What do you think the root of the problem is?" He took her into his arms gently.

"I've lost everyone I ever cared for. I think, maybe, that I'm afraid to be in love, to be so happy. I feel like the more I need you, the more I want to push you away. It doesn't make sense, even to me, but I think there's something there," she smiled shakily. "I think I'm so afraid of losing you that I'm pushing you away to get it over with."

"It's funny how the human mind works. You're pushing me away because you're afraid I'll leave anyway, isn't that strange?" he mused.

"Maybe it's because I feel so dependent on you that something hidden deep inside is ready to surface." She kissed him.

"We'll find out together starting tomorrow, but I think we should drop the subject until we have started to work it out with a therapist." He pulled her over on top of him, gently grasping her still tender butt. "We need tonight to please each other."

The magic started again and they stayed there in bed, pleasing each other until both of them were completely worn out. They found out something: A sore ass doesn't bother you very much, not when you're making love.

Okay you caught me, it really is a self-portrait, but it's really exaggerated. I don't fight that well. My lover is very grateful for that fact, and so is his nose.

Eleven

The Beast: Beauty In The Barn

Another excerpt from my novel: <u>The Heart of the Beast</u>. A new take on <u>Beauty and the Beast</u>, it is a romance novel, not a purely spanking novel but it has several spanking scenes. Somehow, I do not think it will ever be made into a children's film. In this scene, the Beast is restless and has sent for a woman to be brought to him from town. I wonder why Beauty gets upset at that?

The maid, Gwyneth, did the best she could with the woman tied to the master's bed. She set about ripping off the woman's clothes, cleaning the woman up and preparing her for the Beast but she disapproved of the situation. Gwyneth had no words to say to Beauty when she walked into the chamber and saw the naked girl tied to the bed, being readied for the Beast's arrival. So she just gave Beauty a sad look and left the room, quickly and silently.

Beauty was hurt and stunned to see the lass in the bed and almost as afraid as the bound and gagged woman was. She had not yet admitted to herself that she cared for the Beast, yet this woman's presence felt like a dagger in her heart. She barely had time to react when the Beast walked in.

The Beast was truly confounded by Beauty's reaction. First and foremost, she was hurt as if he'd betrayed her, even though there were no marriage vows between them and never would be. Then there was the anger simmering just below the surface as if she were ready to explode. She stood there staring at him for several minutes, never saying a word. Her eyes did her talking for her and they spoke volumes. Finally, she asked the Beast in a very cold and stiffly formal voice if she could leave the castle and return to her home.

"But why Beauty?" the Beast asked completely puzzled. "Why would you want to break your vow? Why would you want to leave me?"

"I'm not staying here to watch you carry on with another woman!" Beauty's temper flared quickly but she struggled to hold on to it.

"Why?" The question was low and ominous. "What do you care if I bed another woman? Remember, you did not wed me, you sold yourself to me for your brother's life. You are not my wife, truly wed before God. You are just a possession, like my falcon or my horse. By what right do you have any say in what I do? Why would you care?"

"Idiot! You mangy cur of a man!" Beauty's control snapped completely. "I am not a sword or a horse. I am a woman who did what she had to do to save her brother. No man owns me. And no man uses me then goes from sharing my bed to sleeping with another woman, not even the mighty Beast!"

She slapped him sharply across the face and trod sharply on his foot, then drew back her leg to kick his shin; her hand reaching for the small dirk she wore at her waist, before she realized what she had done. She had attacked the Beast!

Both of them stood there stunned and shocked for a long moment before, with a sharp cry, Beauty gathered up her skirts and ran. She made it down the stairs and into the great hall before the Beast followed in a rage. He ran, catching Beauty just outside the great wooden door.

As soon as Gwyneth saw the Beast follow Beauty she took some initiative for one of the few times in her life. Smiling, she went upstairs and untied the helpless woman. She gave her a few coins and sent her back to the village with Seth to accompany her.

Furious, the Beast dragged Beauty kicking, punching and cursing him, into the stables and threw her down into the straw. She looked up at him and berated him with words he was shocked to hear falling from her lips. Indeed, he was shocked to learn that she even knew such words, even though he used them often himself. Standing over her, he reached for his belt.

"Nay!" Beauty pleaded, tears streaming down her face. "You promised, not the belt, not ever again!"

The Beast gave a mighty roar of frustration before his fierce anger left him. Looking down at Beauty, he remembered his promise. Few would call him an honorable man, but when he made a vow, he kept it. With considerable effort, almost a visible effort, he calmed himself down and thought for a moment. He soon realized that Beauty was jealous of the village woman and he became secretly pleased by Beauty's reaction to the maiden.

A long-abandoned and nearly forgotten devilish streak took the place of his anger. Lowering himself to the clean, fresh straw beside her, he pulled her atop his lap, rolled her over, lifted her skirts and began to spank her lightly and playfully, and tickle her. He covered her bottom with loud, stinging slaps without an excess of force behind them.

The spanking was more love play than anger, so it wasn't very harsh. Nevertheless, Beauty's bare bottom began to blush a becoming pink. He leaned over to nip one pink cheek. She yelled angrily at him, kicking and calling him names as she struggled to get free.

As she struggled, she got her mouth filled with straw and she had to spit it out in a very unladylike manner in order to continue to berate him. Suddenly the struggling, shrieking and cursing, not to mention the unmistakable sound of slaps connecting with bare skin, drew an observer. Beauty's brother Tom was working in the stables, as he had since Beauty had been at the castle.

"What are you doin' to my sister?" Tom bellowed, his love for Beauty overcoming his common sense and blinding him to his fear and hatred of the Beast.

"What does it look like?" the Beast yelled back as he continued to spank Beauty; indeed, the slaps became quite a bit harder now that there was a witness. "This hoyden actually had the nerve to strike me! She even drew her dagger on me!"

"Beauty! You struck the Beast? Threatened him with your

dagger? Are you crazy? He could have you hung for that!" Tom was shocked to the core.

"He deserved it!" Beauty screamed. "It was one thing when he just told me he was thinking of taking another woman to his bed. I thought I was angry then but now... now he actually has some strumpet in the bedchamber stripped naked and tied to the bed. Now I know what real anger is!"

"Beauty!" Tom was even more shocked. "Are you jealous? Is that possible? Have you come to care for him that much? Have you forgotten who he is?"

"Fool! You're as daft as he is!" Beauty gasped as the smart spanking continued. "Jealous of the Beast! How could I be jealous? This lout thinks I'm just another possession like his horse or his dog."

"More like a bitch," the Beast said roughly, staying his hand for a moment as he asked, "Are ye jealous lass?"

"Nay!" Beauty spat out the answer.

"Are you?" His voice dropped ominously and the spanking resumed; in fact his hands came down a little faster and harder.

"Dolt! Idiot!" she yelled, still squirming and struggling to get away. "Bastard!"

"Are you jealous of me, lass?" His tone was implacable as he spanked a little harder still.

Beauty stopped squirming and turned her head to look back at the Beast. "Please M'lord. I am not jealous of you. How could I be? By your own words, I'm just a possession like your horse. Is your horse jealous when you ride another?"

"Since when has my horse been as difficult to get along with as you are, and given me trouble the way you do?" the Beast mused aloud, laughing. "Mayhap there is some difference between you and my horse. I'll admit that you are much more fun to ride."

The spanking abruptly stopped.

There was a long moment in which no one spoke before the Beast quietly said, "Leave us, Tom."

As Tom hesitated, the Beast repeated more firmly, "Your

sister's all right, man. Now go. Leave us!"

Tom paused to take a quick look at Beauty's red bottom. "You're right M'lord. I myself used to spank her harder than that when she was a fractious child."

"Traitor!" Beauty snarled. "Men!"

"As you can see Tom, she's still fractious, although she's no child." The Beast grinned at Tom, something he'd never done before, quietly repeating a third time, "Leave us."

Tom met the Beast's eyes and for the first time in as long as he could remember, felt some hope for Beauty's future. There was a slight easing of the hatred in Tom's heart, a small lessening of his thirst for vengeance. A tenuous smile passed between the two men. It was the tiniest hint of a truce between them. The universal and timeless acknowledgment amid men throughout the world about the vagaries of a woman's nature. One male agreeing silently with another over the problems caused by a woman. Without another word Tom turned and left, locking the barn door behind him.

As soon as Tom left, the Beast rolled Beauty over. He ignored her soft gasp as her tender bottom found the rough straw. He grasped both of her hands in one of his and held her arms over her head.

He grinned and lowered his mouth to hers whispering gently, "Is it true lass? Are ye jealous? Have you come to care so much for me?"

"Of course not, you fool," Beauty said very softly, but her eyes were soft and half-closed, her breath was coming slowly, and there was the hint of a smile playing on her lips.

"Little liar," whispered the Beast, grinning as he reached for her and gathered her to his arms; he kissed her gently and began to remove her clothes. "I thought you were always truthful."

She met his passion with a need of her own, matching kiss for kiss and caress for caress. He played with her with his mouth and hands before thrusting his manhood deep into her and bringing her to a furious climax.

"It seems there's another difference between you and my

horse," the Beast mused aloud, teasing Beauty. "My horse doesn't get as much pleasure from being ridden as you seem to."

"I but feign my pleasure to boost M'lord's fragile ego," Beauty said primly.

"Feigned?" the Beast teased softly. "You bit my shoulder."

"I was exceedingly hungry," Beauty said sternly, her eyelids almost closed. "Tis long past time for the noon meal."

Those were the last coherent words she said for a very long time as the Beast took her yet again. Later, still lying in the hay, Beauty snuggled contentedly in his arms.

"Why is it that whenever either one of us gets jealous," she ignored his derisive snort and continued, "I'm the one who always winds up with a sore bottom?"

"That's the way of things, Beauty," the Beast grinned, teasing her. "Luckily for me."

The pair put their clothes on and made their way back to the castle. Heads held high, they walked past several soldiers who noticed the dirt and straw sticking to Beauty's torn blue silk gown, and to the Beast's shirt and hose. They walked past servants who noted the bits of straw in their hair and their dirty faces. They headed up the stairs and straight to the bedchamber. Neither one of them noticed the absence of the woman who had been tied to the bed. The Beast ordered Gwyneth to send their supper and hot bathwater up to the bedchamber as soon as possible. He wanted this private time with Beauty to continue.

Soon they were squeezed into the bronze tub together, soaping each other. A large tray of food was placed within reach. There was roast chicken, candied peaches, bread, cheese and fine red wine.

"M'lord?" Beauty ventured timidly, holding a slice of the peach up to his mouth. "Why would you be interested in any other woman? What am I lacking? Do I not do anything you ask? Am I not compliant with your every wish?"

He took a bite and poured a single goblet of wine, drinking from it himself before holding it up to her lips.

"Beauty, you do indeed do everything I ask, and you are very amenable. That may be part of the problem. If you go on being so compliant, you may begin to bore me." The Beast looked at Beauty and demanded, only partly teasing, "Where is the woman who stood up to me in spite of her obvious fear and bargained for her brother's life?"

"Wouldn't I be breaking the agreement if I quibbled with you and argued all the time?" Beauty asked as she reached over and tore a leg off the chicken.

"You agreed to love me and to do anything I asked. Telling me your true feelings on things won't break the agreement. Don't you think wives who love their husbands ever speak back?" the Beast asked, taking the chicken leg from her and eating it himself.

Silently she tore off the other leg and held it out of his reach as she ate it quickly.

"You want me to speak back to you? To fight with you?" Beauty asked as soon as she swallowed her food, astonished to the core.

"Nay, but I want your honesty and I don't think I have it yet. It makes me distrust you," the Beast told her, handing her the goblet of wine.

"You think I'm disloyal? I've done everything you asked without question. What more can I do?" Beauty was puzzled as she sipped her wine.

"You misunderstand, lass. I know you to be completely loyal to me. But I also want you to be true to yourself whilst serving me. I saw the real you once, terrified and pleading, but still you stood toe to toe with me and bargained with me. I'd like to see that lass again," the Beast gazed at her.

"Really?" Beauty's voice was deceptively soft. "How could I bring out that innocent girl, with a mind of her own and just barely enough courage to speak her piece? How, I ask you, when every time I disagree with you or displease you in any small way, I wind up over your knees with a stinging bottom?"

"And you probably always will," the Beast grinned openly before reaching for a crust of bread.

"Why?" Beauty puzzled.

"Because I enjoy taking you over my knees. I enjoy spanking you and making you squirm. I love to see the color come into your cheeks and feel the heat where my hand has been," the Beast smirked watching the color come onto her cheeks. "Not hurting you, mind you, but playing with you."

"Oh? Sometimes your play does smart and sting quite a bit," Beauty said quietly, wishing she wasn't blushing.

"Sometimes I really am punishing you, and sometimes my temper gets away from me," the Beast admitted. "Still, if you want to hold my interest you'll have to find a way to stand up to me once in a while."

"Or?" she asked with quiet dignity.

"Or I'll send you home." The Beast's voice was deceptively steady and firm.

Although it was delivered in a flat, calm voice it was an empty threat. The Beast would never send Beauty away and though neither had admitted it yet, even to themselves, they both knew it. By now the Beast had all but forgotten the oath he'd forced out of Beauty. The oath that she was never to see her family again.

Suddenly Beauty exploded in magnificent anger, shocking the Beast. "Now if that isn't just like a man! If I do what you want, I'm too boring. If I argue, I get punished. Then to top it all, if I bore you, you'll send me home to see the family that I love so much I was willing to die to save one of them. What a stupid threat! Only a man could be so dumb! If I argue and get punished, not only do I lose any hope of seeing my family but I also have to stay here with you! And what have you ever done to make me want to stay with you anyway? Threaten me? Spank me? Rape me? Use me as the lowest servant? I'd sure miss all that if I went back to my loving family, wouldn't I?"

She drank deeply from the wine goblet before pouring more and downing that too.

Shocked, the Beast responded with a rage of his own. "What have I done to make you want to stay? I've treated you better than I ever have any woman before. Your chores are few and easy. Your beatings are not severe at all, I'm almost gentle with you."

His eyes narrowed ominously as she snorted. "I try to give you all the loving that I can. What more do you want?"

"I want the right to disagree with you, even argue. I want to share laughter with you and offer you comfort when things aren't going well for you. I want what I offered you. I want your affection when we make love as much as your passion. I want to be free to see my family and to be trusted to return to you." Beauty paused before continuing softly, "And I want two more things: I want to know what happened to leave the lass named Molly crippled and pregnant… "

"And?" the Beast growled lowly.

"And I want to know what would become of me and the child if I were to become with child," Beauty whispered softly.

"That's quite a list of desires, my love." Both of them tried to ignore his use of the term, even though it was the first time he'd ever addressed her so affectionately. Outwardly, only a brief flicker of shock in her eyes acknowledged that Beauty had even heard it. Inwardly her heart threatened to beat its way out of her chest.

Finally the Beast recovered from his own shock and continued, "I do not know what I would do if you were with child. If you had any noble blood, I could marry you so the child would be my heir."

"What?" Beauty almost shrieked.

She was so astonished that she dropped the goblet into the rapidly cooling bathwater.

"Why not? I have no desire to tie myself to any woman but I do need an heir. One woman is as good as another," the Beast shrugged, grabbing the wine goblet and drinking directly from it, then spitting it out when he realized it was filled with bathwater.

He refilled the goblet from the bottle on the table. "The only difference I can see would be her title and her dowry. If you had those things you would do me as well as any other, nay even better, for I know you and have trained you to my ways. Well, almost trained you."

Beauty fumed as a longing she didn't want to admit, even to herself, filled her soul. She wanted no man to marry her on those terms, she decided. She wanted the man she was to marry to be doing it for only one reason, because he wanted her as his mate for life. Something that would never happen now that she'd given her future to the Beast. Wisely, she kept her feelings to herself. It was only one of her many secrets.

Without knowing her turn of mind, the Beast continued, "But as it is, I do not know. I still refuse to give you permission to visit your family. As for the rest, you are arguing with me right now or hadn't you realized it? And I notice you did not ask me to stop spanking you, or did you forget to mention it?"

"I do not mind it so much," Beauty blushed as she admitted, "as long as you love me afterwards. It's only after you spank me that you open up and really talk to me and cuddle me, like you are now."

She wiggled against him as she continued, "I didn't like the belt though, as it stings and hurts exceedingly."

"You minx!" the Beast exclaimed, as her foot gently explored and teased his burgeoning manhood.

Then he faltered, "About the girl Molly. Yes, as is my right, I took her. At least, I probably did. I really don't remember her. Then I must have left her, maybe to attend to a squabble in the village or handle a crisis in the stables. I don't recall. I just know I didn't cause her injuries. I know I've done many things you disapprove of but I swear to you, before God, I've never done that kind of injury to any woman. I know some men enjoy violence as much as they do sex. I do not."

The statement had the righteousness of truth behind it. "I can only guess what happened. I probably left her in the great hall unguarded. Someone must have dragged her into the barn, raped her and beat her senseless, leaving her crippled. I know not who. I would have wanted her to stay with me so that Gwyneth could care for her, if I had known aught of her injuries." He paused before admitting, "I do know that girls have been attacked after

148

being here, even though I started sending an escort to see them home. That's why you're always so well guarded."

"So you only raped her?" Beauty accused.

"It wasn't rape. If I had her, it was my right. The villagers are mine! Their women are mine!" the Beast shot back. "It's how I was raised."

"I know," Beauty admitted, "but I still can't believe it's morally right."

"We'll argue about that later." The Beast pulled her to him. "Right now I have better ideas. Let's leave this tub and get into that bed."

"Tired, M'lord? 'Tis early," Beauty teased.

"I'm not a bit tired, as you'll soon find out." The Beast gathered her into his arms and dropped her, dripping wet, on the bed. He grabbed the last of the candied peaches from the tray and spread them, artistically, on Beauty's breasts.

"I think I'll have dessert now," he grinned, lowering his mouth to nibble on the sweet fruit.

"Whatever M'lord wishes," Beauty murmured, her eyes closing in passion as she savored the feel of his tongue on her breasts.

"M'lord, I also crave dessert," Beauty moaned as the sensations washed over her.

Reaching out one arm, she grasped the bowl of candied peaches. She pushed against the Beast's muscled chest until he lay back on the mattress. Beauty poured some of the peaches on his chest and began to nibble and suckle until the fruit was removed. The Beast nearly went wild. She poured some more of the fruit onto his erect maleness and ate that right off his body. This time the Beast did go wild, his whole body buckled under her tender, sensual ministrations.

As his breathing returned to normal, the Beast reached out for the bowl of fruit. "'Tis my turn, you've already had two portions," he said gruffly.

He poured the fruit onto the juncture of her thighs and put the bowl aside. Slowly, with his eyes holding hers, he grinned. That grin sent shivers down her spine. However those shivers were nothing compared to the sensations that followed. He lowered his mouth to the tangle of curls and drove her out of her mind. Before he finished driving her to the heights of ecstasy, he had her legs resting on her shoulders, her heels around the back of his neck. She clenched her thighs so hard when she climaxed, she almost strangled him. For once, after her orgasm, he was the one struggling to catch his breath.

As soon as she slowed her own breathing and brought it under control she noted this, "I'm truly sorry, M'lord." She giggled, "I hope I've done you no harm."

I've always enjoyed a quick roll in the hay, a nice bubble bath and supper in bed. And of course, great sex. And I've always enjoyed the challenge that comes from an arrogant, sexy man. Is it just me?

Twelve

Office Pranks, Office Spanks

If you steal company funds, you might be given a choice: submit to company punishment or be fired. Could this happen behind closed doors in an office? A deal that could send you to hell, or could it possibly be heaven?

Martin Colman leaned back in his plush office chair, lost in deep thought about his new secretary, Sandy Denson. Thinking about Sandy was not a new activity for him, he'd been doing it quite a lot lately. Sandy had been working for him just six weeks, and for those six weeks, whenever there was a spare minute, Martin thought about her, daydreamed about her, fantasized about her.

To be truthful, he sometimes found himself acting like a green schoolboy and masturbating while thinking about her. Hot thoughts. Erotic thoughts. Triple-X rated thoughts. That kind of fantasizing was something Martin hadn't done in years, not since he was a horny teenager.

He hadn't had to. Martin had plenty of friends and almost any woman he wanted. He was 35, about 6'2" with a lean, athletic build, sun-streaked light brown hair, blue eyes, a dimple and perfect teeth that he showed often because he was always smiling. He had a friendly, easygoing personality and that smile was real and warm.

Women found him attractive and men thought he was a great guy. He was well spoken and polite, almost gentle. He was intelligent but not an intellectual snob. He didn't drink to excess or use any drugs. He was open and outgoing, and had a great sense of humor. He was, in fact, the kind of man most women dream about but never really meet.

He was also successful. He was a very busy accountant and junior partner at the large firm of Smithson and Broyer, one of their youngest junior partners ever.

He was all that, and still there he sat thinking about Sandy. Not that it was an unusual pastime for him; since whatever gods or fates resided in the personnel department had sent him Sandy, Martin had spent a great deal of his time thinking about her. What man wouldn't?

Sandy was extremely beautiful. She had a perfect oval face with high cheekbones, a full mouth and bright, blue eyes like Martin himself, only hers were even bluer. Her hair was usually pulled back into a tight, stylish bun. The kind of bun that should have made her look like an old maid, but it didn't. It was rare for her to wear it down but when she did let it down, it was almost waist length, wavy, the color of honey and sun-streaked. All this was matched by a body to die for: Her breasts were large and full but not too extreme; they just seemed to fit her build. She also had a small waist, rounded hips, great buns and long shapely legs.

She was quite possibly the most beautiful woman he had ever seen. Not that he was biased, Martin thought to himself ruefully, and he sure wasn't infatuated with her either, well not too much.

The attraction Martin was fighting wasn't just based on her looks either, as she was also beautiful within. She always had a smile, a kind word or an intelligent comment. She was warm, friendly and quietly efficient. Very smart. She dressed well and acted very professionally.

She even matched Martin's off beat sense of humor. She seemed to brighten up the office. When personnel sent her to him for an interview, he felt like he had won the lottery.

There was just one problem.

The problem had nothing to do with her work; she was as good as a secretary as she was beautiful. She worked well with Martin and they just blended into a team. She never complained about anything she was asked to do; instead she rarely seemed to need any direction to know what Martin needed to have done.

She was fast and efficient, and always willing to do anything she could to help Martin do a better job. She made intelligent suggestions and would offer impartial comments when he asked her opinion. Her shorthand, rare these days, was excellent, as were her typing and spelling. She was also a whiz with a computer. Sometimes she almost made Martin feel unnecessary, as if she could do both their jobs without him.

Martin had lots of time to daydream too. They were in a fairly slack time of year. Just before Sandy became his secretary Martin had been very busy; he had been responsible for several major projects that had to be finished before the annual stockholder's meeting. He had worked long and hard, putting in seemingly endless overtime. To top it off, he did all that work with the dubious aid of his former secretary.

Judy was a nice girl, sweet and pretty, but she had not been a distraction to Martin's focus on work. She was not able to keep up with Martin's work pace either. Martin had been very happy when she came to him and said that she was getting married and tendered her resignation. He was relieved he wasn't faced with the awkward necessity of firing her.

Now with Sandy, there was a problem. The problem was that Martin found himself in a dilemma. Nowadays, sexual harassment was a very widespread issue. There was lots of real harassment of course, but there was also the other extreme. The time for innocent flirtations, for friendships and even budding office romances was past. Some fairly innocuous remarks often led one office worker to file complaints against another with management, resulting in witch-hunts and destroyed reputations. This climate of constraint had Martin in a quandary. He wanted to have that office romance. He wanted Sandy, both in his bed and in his life. His problem was: how was he going to get passed a straight employer/employee relationship and into a romance without crossing the bounds into sexual harassment?

If he did manage to get passed that formal barrier with Sandy, how would he know if she really cared for him or if she felt forced into a relationship she didn't really want by his authority over her?

Normally Martin was rather adept at reading a woman's subtle signs. He usually knew if an advance would be welcome or not. However it was different with Sandy. Martin was hampered by the fact that her office demeanor was always friendly, but also cool and professional. She was rather formal in the office, almost too polite and respectful. She gave him no hint, no impression that she felt anything for him other than as her boss. Even though he asked her to call him Martin, she still called him Mr. Colman.

It was too bad Martin didn't realize how hard it was for Sandy to maintain her professional demeanor. Every time he walked through the office she clenched her hands into fists to keep from reaching for him. When he smiled and praised her work, her face felt frozen in a cool professional mask. He never had a clue that her pulse was racing, and sometimes her panties were getting wet. Half of her office formality was the result of her efforts at suppressing her attraction to him. There was no way she was going to risk the best job she had ever had by coming on to the boss.

He had never even heard her say his first name in the office. She had said it once at the office picnic. She had been there with her daughter, an eight-year-old beauty named Kelsey. Martin had joined Kelsey and Sandy at their picnic table and ran a three-legged race with Kelsey. When they'd won the race, Sandy had called him Martin.

Later that day Martin was sitting next to her in the bleachers during the company softball game, and when the little girl hit a home run Sandy got so excited she gave Martin a hug. They both were surprised by the spark of electricity that flowed in the brief contact. It had been enough to trigger secret fantasies for both of them. It had given each of them a tiny bit of hope.

The next day she went back to her slightly formal office demeanor. Neither one of them had followed up on that spark yet. So far so good, Martin thought, ignoring his nagging suspicion that he was halfway in love with her and all the way to acting like a gawky teenager.

Martin ached to change that atmosphere without losing his most efficient secretary ever. Sandy came in after Judy quit and turned his office around. She was uncanny. Always a step ahead of him in knowing what should be done next but flexible enough to let him lead the way. Always willing to stay late or come in early. Everything he wanted in a secretary.

Unfortunately, she seemed to be everything he wanted in a woman too. He wanted her in every way: By his side at the office, dining with him in good restaurants or watching TV at home. Most of all, he wanted her beside him in bed all night.

Suddenly the unspoken attraction wasn't the only problem. All of this was minor compared to another, more immediate problem. This new problem was that she was the only possible suspect in the theft of fifteen hundred dollars from the petty cash drawer!

So here was Martin again, sitting at his desk and thinking about Sandy. This time it was a real problem. This time was different however. This time it was a real problem. He was trying to decide what to do about Sandy. After all, she had taken money from the office petty cash fund.

Normally he would have just replaced the funds and then gotten the money back from Sandy. He had every faith that she intended to return it, she was no thief. He instinctively knew she must have had a good reason for taking it. This wasn't normal though because old Mr. Smithson himself had discovered the theft in a random audit. Martin had been so surprised that he had failed to think up a cover story.

Martin could see no easy way out of it. Mr. Smithson wanted Sandy fired and prosecuted. Martin was trying to think of a way to avoid that catastrophe. He wanted to keep Sandy. Mr. Smithson ordered Martin to have her arrested too. Martin had to find a way to help Sandy restore the money, and then penalize her in some way that would get old Mr. Smithson off his back. He didn't want Sandy fired or thrown in jail. Most of all, he wanted to keep her as his secretary.

Sandy arrived at the office that morning completely unaware of the effect she had on Martin. She knew he liked her but she had no idea how far it had gone. She worked hard to keep that faint air of formality between them because she privately thought there was no more pathetic, scheming creature on the face of the earth than a secretary who threw herself at her boss. Especially when said boss was extremely handsome, friendly and very likable.

That Monday it was easy not to think about how likable Martin, Mr. Colman, was; all her thoughts were centered on something else. One thing. Her only thought was to talk to Martin about the money she had borrowed and hope he would understand. She wanted to make an arrangement for repaying it. She had always meant to repay. She hoped Martin would let her keep her job.

Martin decided to talk to Sandy first. After all, a girl with her impressive references had to have some reason for doing something so stupid.

He buzzed her on the intercom. "Sandy, come in here please."

She entered his office slowly. She knew she was in trouble the moment she looked at his face. There was such a cold look in his eyes. She took a deep breath and went to stand in front of him. She had been trying to figure out how to tell him what she had done all morning. How to explain. She wondered if he would help her or if she would be fired. She decided to tell him straight out, whether he knew about the missing money or not. She hoped he would be able to help her stay out of trouble.

Before Martin could say a word she said, "Mr. Colman, I have to talk with you for a moment. I don't know how to say it. I'm very ashamed, but I did something terribly wrong and if there's a way I can make it right, I will do whatever it takes." She paused, "I…"

"Shut up!" Martin said harshly. "Do not say another word."

He picked up the phone, dialing Mr. Smithson's extension. "Mr. Smithson, she's here." He listened for a moment. "Yes sir, as soon as she walked in." He listened again. "Before I said a word." He listened once more. "Please. Let me handle

156

everything. Sir, if I can get a voluntary confession and full restitution... " Another pause. "Punish her?" He sounded surprised. "I'll call you later for your approval. Okay."

Hearing this, Sandy shook visibly; she realized he knew all about it. He hung up the phone and turned to face Sandy.

He looked up at Sandy. "Mr. Smithson himself decided to do a spot audit last weekend. Can you guess what he found?" He watched as Sandy went deathly pale.

"I thought I'd be able to put it back today," Sandy said softly, she met his eyes directly and tried not to let her fear show. "Three times my ex-husband Phil told me he had already sent the money and three times he was lying."

"So you did steal the petty cash, didn't you, Sandy?" he asked abruptly.

"I only meant to borrow it. I... "

"Don't tell me why you took the money. Tell me how you're going to pay it back before end of business today," Martin said sternly.

"Let me call Phil," Sandy requested. "Maybe he can bring it to me."

At Martin's nod she went to her desk and made the call. Before long she returned to stand in front of him. "He told me he changed his mind and decided to take a trip to Vegas this weekend instead of mailing me the money," she admitted softly. "That's the same money he previously said he had already mailed. He said he hoped I'd go to jail so he could get custody of Kelsey."

"Do you see how much trouble you got into for believing him?" Martin asked.

At her shy nod he went on, "Will you make full restitution by Friday at the end of business?"

Again she nodded without a word.

"Mr. Smithson wants me to fire you and send you to jail," Martin said sadly. "He said he would fire me if I tried to cover for you, otherwise I'd put the money back and you could pay me."

"Should I call the police for you?" There was a tremor in her voice.

"No," Martin said softly, "not before we talk. Maybe not at all. Sit down please and let's see if I can keep you out of jail."

"Thank you Mr. Colman," Sandy said as she sat in front of his desk.

"Call me Martin," he replied almost instinctively.

"I can't," Sandy said surprised. "It's much too informal!"

"If you can steal from me, you can use my first name," Martin pointed out. "Theft is a bigger break in office decorum."

"Borrow!" Sandy protested.

"Whatever." He continued, "Will you sign a full confession, one that includes the provisions for restitution?"

"Yes, sir." Her voice was low, almost a whisper, her head down.

"Then you can pay it back?" Martin probed.

"I will!" Sandy said firmly. "I swear, but not now."

"Good." Martin paused. "Sandy, you know that would be good enough for me, but Mr. Smithson got involved and things are not that simple for him. He said you must be, in his words, punished severely. He recommends jail, which I don't want because I don't want to lose you as my secretary."

"Thank you." Sandy sounded shaky.

"So I'm proposing an alternative. You are going to sign the confession and written plans for full restitution including interest. Last, but not least, will you voluntarily submit to company disciplinary measures? That is if we agree in writing not to report this to the police after the discipline is carried out?" He was stern.

"What sort of disciplinary measures?" she asked quietly, submissively and a bit warily.

"I don't know for sure yet. That's the first part of the punishment. I want you to make a list of at least six different forms of disciplinary measures we can use against you, and have them on my desk for me to look over by lunch at the latest," he told her. "I will decide what to do."

"What kind of things could I think of?" Sandy was puzzled.

"You mean like, ah, being fired? A cut in pay? That sort of thing?"

"Yes, that's it." It took the pressure off of Martin to come up with the ideas for company sanctions.

"Those are the only two that come to mind." She was perplexed.

"Then think harder; if you don't have all six on my desk by one o'clock this afternoon, the cops will be here at one fifteen," he threatened coldly. "Be sure to type up the confession first and bring it in here for my approval before you and I both sign it."

"I will, Mart..., I mean Mr. Colman," Sandy said. "Thank you for giving me a chance."

She left the room and went back to her desk. She quickly typed up a short confession. Then she began to think of ways he could punish her and how she could pay back the money.

A short while later, she brought in the required confession and handed it to him timidly. He read it over carefully and approved it. She signed the form and he witnessed it.

Sandy brought in her punishment list just before lunch and handed it to Martin. It read:

```
1. I get fired
2. I take a pay cut
3. I work overtime for free
4. I lose my company parking space
5. I lose use of the executive washroom
6. I lose use of the executive lunchroom
```

She took the list in to Martin and placed it in front of him. He read the list carefully and picked up a pencil, quickly crossing off several items. The list, when he handed it back to her, had quick little notations on it. The list now looked like this:

```
1. I lose my last raise
2. I    lose    the    perks    of    an    executive
   secretary:
   a. My parking space
   b. Executive washroom
   c. Executive lunchroom
3.
4.
5.
6.
```

"Try again, I need four more ideas," Martin said coldly, not mentioning the one Mr. Smithson himself had offered. He wanted her to come up with that one all on her own. "Have it on my desk within the hour. And Sandy," he paused until she met his gaze, "don't bother including anything that causes me to lose you as my personal secretary."

In a very short time she brought him a new list. It read:

```
1. I lose my last raise
2. I lose all executive privileges
3. My lunch hour is cut to a half hour
4. I pay the company a fine, over and above
   payback of what I took
5. I work overtime for free
6. I lose my seniority
```

She took the list to Martin again. He was on the phone. In his ear, Mr. Smithson was saying, "Keep rejecting something on the list until she suggests it herself, and I want to look at it the next day, to see proof."

Without a word, Martin took the list. "Everything's okay except for the lunch hour thing, and for you losing your seniority. It would be too hard for personnel to keep covered up. I need a full hour for lunch so you have to take a full hour. I can't leave you in the office alone, at least not for a while. Try again."

He crossed off number 3 and number 5. "Now," he said

coldly, handing the revised sheet to her, "finish the list and make it quick."

A short while later she returned, worried. "Sir, I came up with one more idea, but I honestly can't think of any more."

"Let's see." He looked at the revised list, she had added:

```
1. I get sent back to the steno pool
```

"That's no good because I would still lose you as my secretary, but I will leave it on the list, temporarily. Now think of a sixth."

"I'm just surprised you didn't want me to add sleeping with my boss to the list," Sandy muttered. Then she looked up and said, "Forget I said that please. I know you're not the kind of man to try to take advantage like that."

"I probably would be but," Martin grinned wickedly, "I just can't bring myself to think of your sleeping with me as a punishment for you. Foolish of me maybe."

"Oh! It wouldn't be," Sandy said quickly. "I've always thought we… " She flushed, "Let me go work on the list."

When she returned she handed him a new list. It read:

```
1. I lose my last raise
2. I lose all executive privileges
3. I lose the matching contributions to my
   employee savings plan.
4. I pay the company a fine, over and above
   payback of what I took
5. I work overtime for free,
6. I
```

"I can't think of anything else," she said softly.

"Then think out loud," Martin said sternly. How are people punished"?

"Jail, or fines, or community labor." She looked at him hopefully.

"No, I mean punished by us, not the community. Go on how are people punished?"

"Well in the good old days, people were, no I mean kids were… " her voice trailed off.

"Were what?" Martin asked sharply.

"Spanked!" Sandy blushed. "But that's silly, surely you wouldn't… "

"I would," Martin said coldly. "Add it to the list. No. Wait." He paused and stared at her. "Pull up the confession on my computer, then go back to your own desk and wait for me. You might try to do something useful, like work, while you're waiting if you don't mind."

"Yes sir." She quickly pulled up the file she had put her confession in and left the room.

After she left, he picked up the phone and called his boss. "I did it!" he said excitedly. "And she thinks it was all her idea." He listened for a minute then said, "Yes sir, I will."

He reread the confession before he started entering a new document at the bottom. Finally he was satisfied and pushed print, making two copies. After it printed, he proofread it and deleted the file.

Sandy waited in agony, wondering which punishments he had decided to use. Surely he wouldn't… She pulled herself together. She knew it was his choice; she had no option but to go along with his decision. Whatever it was, it would be better than jail. She heard the printer, then it stopped. It had her confession and the list of punishments as follows:

> I, Sandy Denson, freely confess that I took a sum of $1,500.00 dollars from the discretionary funds of my employer, Smithson and Broyer, on Friday Oct. 15. I did this without obtaining permission from my supervisor, Martin Colman. I agree to repay the funds and submit to the punishment listed below. The punishments I have agreed to submit to are as follows:

1. I will have the money from my last raise put in a special account
2. I will also put the money I get for working overtime in that account
3. I will pay the company back when the fund equals a total of one and a half times the amount I took, which would be $2,250.00
4. I lose the matching contributions to my employee savings plan until that time
5. I lose all executive privileges
6. I will submit, without protest, to severe corporal punishment from my supervisor, Mr. Colman; I will follow his instructions in the matter of my punishment.

I realize that these terms are subject to the approval of Mr. Smithson and that upon completion of these terms, the company will drop any threat of prosecution.

Martin took the document to Sandy to sign. She read it quickly and snorted once before signing it.

"Okay Sandy, what was that very unladylike snort about?" Martin asked sternly.

"I have to submit to severe corporal punishment *without protest?*" she questioned. "Submit, well okay, but without protest? You must be kidding."

"Don't worry about it Sandy, I simply meant that there was to be no quibbling or reluctance. However screams, gasps and moans are all allowed," Martin said coldly before he turned away so she wouldn't see his smile. "Just no swearing."

"Oh well then," she said with a touch of sarcasm, "that's all right." She paused and continued in a soft tone, "Mr. Colman, when... "

"The punishments all go into effect beginning Monday, except for the spanking of course. That will happen immediately, as soon as I get the final approval on this list from old Mr. Smithson, and arrange your pay cut with personnel. They won't know it's a pay cut; to avoid any speculation about it and protect your reputation, I will arrange for the dollar per hour and all the overtime pay to go into a special payroll savings account. Then, when the balance in the account reaches one and a half times what you stole, the company will take it and your full pay will automatically be restored."

"Thank you for saving me that embarrassment," she whispered with a shaky voice.

He paused, then continued, "As for the spanking, I would rather not punish you here in a crowded office. Tonight at five I want you to leave work and go out to buy something for me to use in your spanking." At her gasp, he went on, "I'm not going to hurt my hand. Be at my house with it by six."

"But what can I buy?" she asked puzzled and panicked. "And where?"

"Let me think." Martin paced. "Try that saddle shop on Main Street. They might have a selection of riding crops. Or the sex shop on Third," Martin suggested. "And be sure not to get one of those thin wimpy looking crops. Get a good, solid one."

"Okay, Martin." Sandy seemed subdued.

"And Sandy?" She looked at him. "Do not show up at my place tonight wearing any pantyhose. Understand?" She nodded mutely.

"Now let's get some work done, we're behind schedule." Martin was all business.

He went in his office and called Mr. Smithson.

"Son, you are one lucky dog," the old man said gleefully. "What I wouldn't give to have a nice round bottom like that at my mercy," he chortled. "I may have to be in private conference with my secretary all day just thinking about it. Are you sure you wouldn't let me... "

"No. I'll handle it, sir," Martin said with a smile in his voice. "You sound as if you'd enjoy it too much."

"I'll admit, I do like taking some fine young thing over my

164

knees once in a while and spanking her to a warm, rosy glow. What's wrong with that?"

"Not a thing sir, if the fine young thing is willing," Martin said, trying not to picture old Mr. Smithson with Sandy over his knees. "But I've never tried it."

"Now you will. Phyllis has been over my knees at least once a week for ten years, and on her knees under my desk more often than that," Mr. Smithson said about his long-time secretary. "Of course she's been my lover for almost all that time. Since about a year after I lost my wife."

"She's devoted to you," Martin said, hiding his astonishment.

"And Sandy is to you. Keep her, son. Get her out of just being in your office and into the rest of your life. Beginning at the bottom," Mr. Smithson advised. "And make it hard; I want you to mark her and I want to see the marks in the morning."

"Yes sir," Martin said firmly.

"And enjoy yourself while you're at it!" That sounded remarkably like an order.

Enjoy myself, Martin thought, beating Sandy? I've thought of all kinds of scenarios with her at my mercy, but beating her was never part of it. How can I enjoy myself causing her pain? Maybe I'll have to think this over. With his office door shut, he tried to visualize himself whipping Sandy's pretty bottom. Soon enough, as his pants began to feel tight and uncomfortable, he knew he could do it and enjoy it.

He was ashamed of himself for it, so he hid it, but he was getting excited now. He had never been a sadist, but he couldn't help thinking how it would feel to have Sandy's pretty white ass at his disposal. He wondered if it was true that some girls got turned on by a spanking. Sandy probably wouldn't, he decided, it would have to be much too harsh a spanking. She didn't know it yet, but at Mr. Smithson's insistence he had to leave marks that old Mr. Smithson could still see the following day. He thought about how he was going to punish Sandy all the way home.

Martin was really a gentle man at heart. He didn't want to hurt Sandy and left to his own devices he certainly would have

HOT CROSSED BUNS

handled things differently. He was more than halfway in love with her. He would have found out why she needed the money, repaid it for her, and set up some kind of repayment plan for her to repay him. Since he had no choice however, he decided to enjoy the chance to have her at his mercy, partially naked, if he could. In a flash of guilty self-doubt he wondered if that made him a hypocrite.

Sandy poked her head into his office at five and said, "I'm leaving now, Martin. I will be at your place at six."

"That's fine, Sandy." He paused. "I wish things were different."

"It's not your fault, Martin. It's mine," she said softly. "It'll be all right."

"Are you scared?" he asked since she seemed as calm as ever.

"Yes." She closed the door. "Very scared," she said aloud to herself.

Martin went home and made some preparations. He was not into S & M, but he had been on the receiving end of some rather severe strapping as a boy. He knew the drill. First, he changed into a worn pair of jeans and a polo shirt. He quickly put some stew he'd made the day before on the stove to warm up, and made sure he had chilled wine. He also put a small bowl of water with a washcloth in it in the refrigerator to chill.

Then he went into the dining room. He moved all the chairs away from the dining table, putting one of the armless wooden chairs in the center of the room. He took everything off the table, setting things on the sideboard in a careless heap. He went outside and came back in with a length of soft rope. He checked on the stew, turning off the heat. Then he sat in his living room and waited.

After going into the ladies' lounge and removing her pantyhose, Sandy left the office. She noticed a certain wetness while she was in the lounge. Could she be aroused? She asked herself. This was no laughing matter; she knew Martin had no choice. He had to make it hurt, or Mr. Smithson would never be convinced to drop the prosecution. She considered briefly before deciding to stop at the saddle shop and not the sex store. At least at the saddle shop she could pretend the crop was for use on a horse.

She felt really strange looking over the selection. Most of them were surprisingly brightly colored and the differences in weight and length were surprising. She picked up a solid black crop, fairly thick and about 18 inches long. It had a wide black leather thong on the end. She paid for it without remark and went out to her car. After a moment's hesitation, she drove to Martin's house. She got out of the car and rang his doorbell.

Sandy was at his door shortly before six, with a riding crop in her hand. When Martin opened the door she said, "Buying this when I knew it was for use on my, my, um, well, it was embarrassing as hell."

"I'll bet!" he said, grinning at her. He was trying to appear as though this was normal but it was a facade, he was nervous himself. "At least you're a bit early, as usual. Come on in," Martin greeted her.

She just stood on his doorstep for a moment, her face was pale and she was shaking. She looked nervous and frightened.

Martin reached for her arm and gently but firmly pulled her into the house. With his hand on her arm she walked in and handed him the crop.

He set it down. "Sit down, while you can still sit, and have some wine." He handed her a glass of wine. It was a poor attempt at a joke.

She sat on his living room sofa and accepted the glass of white wine.

"I'm so nervous; can't we just get this over with?" she asked.

"Trust me, Sandy, a glass or two of wine first won't hurt," he told her. "It's not like this is something you're looking forward to."

"No, I'm not," she admitted, sipping the wine.

"Have you got your daughter with a sitter?" he asked.

"No. She's at my mother's house for the night." Sandy finished the glass of wine.

Martin poured her a second glass and poured some more for himself.

167

"Martin, I want you to know why I took the money," she said with amazing dignity.

"No, not until after," Martin said firmly. "I don't want to be sympathetic. I've never been on the giving end of this before. I haven't even been on the receiving end since I was about thirteen." He paused. "Sandy, I have to use that crop hard enough to leave visible marks tomorrow. Mr. Smithson would only agree to this arrangement if he can check you for bruises in the morning. He demanded it, or there's no deal. He'll just call the police and have you arrested. Do you understand?"

"It's okay. I got myself into this, and I want to do anything I can to get myself out of it." She blushed, "There is one problem though, I've never been spanked, not even by my own parents. So I'm afraid that I'll struggle or run, or put my hands in the way or something. That I won't be able to stand it. Not to be disobedient, you understand, but because I can't help myself. I'm more afraid of doing something foolish than I am of the pain." She grinned weakly, "Well, almost."

He finished his wine. Then he stood up and walked over to the straight-backed wooden chair. "Sandy, come here. Over my knees. I'm sure you're familiar with the position."

"Not from personal experience," she said, gulping the rest of her wine.

She did as he ordered without a word of protest. She walked over to him and very gingerly bent over his knees. He adjusted her position so that she was comfortably situated over his knees and then he stroked her bottom gently.

He spanked her, not very hard at all, right over her navy skirt. Gradually he built up the rhythm and the force. After a short time he raised her skirt and continued spanking her.

The little pink panties underneath did little to conceal her charms. Soon both of them were aware of just how arousing he found her position. His hardness was trapped under her body.

He was barely spanking her really, just a series of teasing little smacks, alternating sides of her bottom. The smacks got harder and made a smacking sound as each one landed on her pert

168

behind. He slid the panties down her shapely legs and then smacked her quite a bit harder; a full dozen, first on one side then the other. Then a full dozen, very hard, right on the center, which stung worst of all. He had her stand up and poured her a third glass of wine.

"Okay, so far?" he asked.

"Of course." She sat without pain and sipped the wine. She was concentrating on not letting her embarrassment show. "That wasn't too bad."

"Good, because I really enjoyed it," Martin grinned, then sobered. "The rest will be worse."

He gave her about ten minutes. "Go get the crop and hand it to me. Ask me to give you a good hard whipping."

Embarrassed, she reluctantly followed his orders. "Please give me a good hard whipping," she muttered.

"Say it again, like you mean it this time," he ordered. "And ask for it on your bare bottom."

She hung her head but said with more emotion, "Please give me a good, hard whipping on my bare bottom."

"Better." He paused. "All right my dear, I will. I will give you a very hard whipping right on your bare bottom. I will make it fiery hot and flaming red for you. Stand at the end of the dining table and wait," he ordered, all business-like. Without a word she did as she was told. He then picked up the ropes.

"Please, don't tie me." She was unable to contain the protest.

"Well, this is going to be a lot worse than a plain spanking. I really need to have you stand still and submit. Are you sure you wouldn't want me to tie you up for the punishment?" he asked gently. "I know from past experience how hard it can be to hold yourself in position for a severe whipping."

Sandy bit her lip and said nothing.

"It's your choice but if you try to evade your punishment in any way, like using your hands to cover your bottom or standing up and moving away from the table, it will cost you more swats. Six each time," Martin said sternly. "And they will be even more severe."

"Okay, use the ropes," Sandy submitted.

Martin ordered her to remove her navy blue blazer, white silk blouse and navy skirt. She did it without protest or question. He also asked her to remove her lacy beige slip. She started to say something but changed her mind and did as he requested.

He had her stand up against the dining room table. He used the rope to tie her hands to the far legs, pulling her down so that she lay on the table. And tied her feet to the legs nearest the end of the table where she stood. She stiffened up as he tied her with the ropes but clinched her lips shut and made no comment. She flinched when he walked over behind her with the crop, but still said nothing.

"I'm going to start with a spanking just like before, to get you warmed up. Then I'm going to crop you. Three dozen strokes. I have to do it hard enough to mark you, so it will hurt. Just remember that this will keep you out of jail. And even prevent you from losing custody of your daughter," Martin said. "Is the wine helping?"

"I think so," she said softly. "I'm ready, Martin. Do it!"

"Well, if you insist," he grinned.

He walked around to stand behind her and pulled down her lacy pink underwear, being careful not to rip them in the process.

He stroked her buttocks gently, exploring. He slid his finger along the crack. When she started to squirm, he stopped stroking her. He gave her a spanking on each cheek, starting easy and building in severity. Each slap made a loud CLAP and caused her buttocks to turn pink. At one point she tensed her buttocks, but she consciously relaxed again after only one harsh slap.

"Told ya so!" he gave a little laugh. "If the hand was all there was, you could probably even enjoy it in a way."

He was rewarded by her little tense laugh.

The spanking continued for several more slaps, and then Sandy began to squirm. He was really in the spirit now, her ass was so pretty and pink. Each slap of his hand was very hard, and they came very fast. He spanked her more firmly and harshly than he had before, hard enough to make her squirm and gasp, hard

170

enough to make her bottom a bright, hot pink before he ever picked up the crop. He realized she was enjoying spanking her. It was a long time before he stopped.

He stopped for a minute and ran his finger into her slit, finding it wet and slippery!

"You have been enjoying this so far!" He rubbed his wet finger on her cheek. "Now get ready for the crop!"

Sandy squirmed against the ropes.

"How does it feel to be tied up and partially naked?" he asked in a gentle tone, genuinely interested. Absently mindedly, he stroked her firm bare bottom.

"Frightening. Embarrassing. Cold," she managed. "I'm scared and I want to put this off but I also want you to go ahead and get it over with."

"Well, when I get through with you you'll be warm enough, believe me. As for whether you want to put this off or get it over with, that's up to me, isn't it?" Martin teased, lightly slapping her ass. "I think I'll leave you this way for about fifteen minutes before I begin."

"Please…"

"Please what?" he asked.

"Nothing, I don't know."

In a few minutes he came over and shocked her by putting a blindfold on her. She opened her mouth to protest but no words came out. He left her again. She waited in nervous agony.

Finally he returned.

He told her, "My parents were firm believers in strict corporal punishment so I was punished like this all too often when I was a boy, without the blindfold, of course. It's really not too awful, but it does hurt. This may be hard, yet it will also help you if you keep the cheeks of your ass relaxed. Remember, I have no choice in the matter. I have to be severe. I need to leave welts or bruises. Are you ready?"

"Are you enjoying this?" she asked, suddenly suspicious.

"In a way. I certainly don't want to cause you any embarrassment or pain. I never have. If it were up to me I

171

wouldn't ever do anything to hurt you. I must admit however, that there is something very arousing about having you tied, naked and at my mercy. Also, while I don't want to hurt you, I am excited about whipping you. I'm ashamed to admit it; that I feel this macho, sexual thrill. It bothers me. I don't know why I'm feeling it; it must be some leftover primitive instinct. How about you? Is there any trace of sexual excitement in this for you?"

"I'm not sure if there is," she said softly, "it's covered by the fear."

"Are you ready?"

"No," she replied, "but go ahead."

He picked up the riding crop and slashed it through the air several times causing a slight whistling sound. The last of his qualms fell away and he felt primitive and merciless.

"Don't tease me!" She sounded almost angry. "Just do it!"

"You may want to rethink that remark in a minute," he laughed in pure joy as he swished the crop through the air again, and then brought it crashing down on her already pink ass.

She screamed.

Martin began the whipping. With the crop he started hard and firm, no warm up. Each stroke was meant to punish and cause pain, and each stroke did just that. CRACK! Her bottom jiggled at the force of the blows. SWISH! CRACK! Each swish of the crop left a trail of bright red lingering in its wake. CRACK! She gave a little cry at each slicing cut of the crop. Martin did not enjoy this as much as he had spanking and humiliating her, he was no real sadist, but he was diligent. After almost thirty strokes he began to realize something.

It didn't seem to raise welts or bruise as much as he had hoped. It seems those crops were designed not to raise welts on the horses.

"Sandy, I'm almost done," he said firmly. "The thing is: this crop isn't leaving the marks I'd hoped to leave. I'm going to finish off the last six with my belt. It will hurt, but as I remember all too well, it will also mark you."

He put down the crop and began to remove his heavy western belt. She shivered at the faint hiss of the belt sliding through the belt loops and tried to mentally brace herself for what was to come. She failed miserably. The first lash of the leather belt caught her unprepared. It landed hard and mercilessly. WHAP! It HURT! It HURT! It left a dark red trail. WHAP! She screamed a full scream. Another stripe appeared. WHAP! Her screams were continuous now, loud and high-pitched. Her whole bottom was bright red and burning with pain. WHAP! God! That one went into the crack of her bottom. Where would the next one land? WHAP! It hit a previous mark. She struggled against the ropes, still screaming. WHAP! The hardest yet. It landed completely on already reddened skin. Martin threw down the belt and untied her. It was over. At least the whipping was.

"Go stand over there facing the wall." He pointed to a spot. Sandy, walking on shaky legs, did as she was told.

Martin lowered the lights except the one that lit up her blazing backside, showing the welts and bruises in exquisite detail. He sat and drank another glass of wine while looking at his handiwork. It took a few moments and at first his hands were shaking, although Sandy never knew it. By the time he finished his wine however, he had relaxed. He stared at her gorgeous backside and realized without any guilt that he had enjoyed himself immensely, in spite of his shaky hands. He walked over to her and gently pulled up her panties.

"Sandy, it's over," Martin said softly. "Come over to the sofa and try to relax."

"Here. That wasn't so bad, was it?" he asked solicitously.

She didn't answer, she just stared at him as if he had three heads.

"I don't want to sit," she finally said softly.

As she turned to face him, he saw that her eyes were moist. The internal war he was fighting between his basic gentle, caring nature and the hidden macho, slightly sadistic male was instantly suspended, at least for the moment. His gentle nature was once again in control.

"Then lie down, Sandy, make yourself as comfortable as you can," he suggested.

"I should dress," she began.

"There's no need, sweetie." The endearment slipped out unnoticed by them both. "There's only the two of us here and I've already seen, I mean, I don't think you need to get dressed on my account. I can control myself."

"I know, Martin," she said softly. She never even noticed her use of his first name. "Your control is perfect, as usual. As long as you don't think I'm trying to... "

"Sandy, you're in pain and the clothes will only make it worse. There's no need to apologize or worry about what I think of you," Martin said firmly. "Lay down, I'll be right back."

He brought her another glass of wine. He sat beside her, talking gently. She drank while sort of lying on her stomach.

"I hate to say this but if I were you I would not use any ice packs or cold cloths to ease the pain. You want those bruises to look as bad as possible tomorrow."

He sat on the end of the sofa so that she could lay with her head in his lap. He cuddled her gently, and if, in a corner of his brain, he thought about how often he'd fantasized about having her head in his lap under different circumstances, who could blame him? He stroked her hair gently and kept speaking to her in a gentle tone.

After a while he went to the kitchen and brought them both some of his homemade stew and a loaf of crusty French bread. After they ate, he took the dishes away and put them in the dishwasher. He came back and once again sat on the sofa with her in his arms.

Finally he asked her the question he'd been waiting to ask. "Can you tell me how it happened? Why you took the money?"

"I'd been out of work for quite a while before I came to work for you. The job market is so bad, it's unreal. Since my divorce, I had saved for five years to buy a house. Finally, I made an offer on one of those homes over on Cedar Ridge. It's not a new home or very large, but it's in good condition and the owner is eager to sell. They accepted my offer but only on condition that I make a down payment of $10,000 by noon on Friday." She looked up at him. "I had $8,500 but they said it wasn't enough. I would have asked for your help but you left early that day. I tried to reach you and even left a message on your machine."

"I'm sorry I wasn't there for you," he whispered softly. "I got in late and I was, um, distracted. I still haven't even checked my messages yet."

"It's not your fault. When the real estate agent called and said that he had to have the money by six, I panicked. I wanted that house so badly. It's perfect for my little girl and me. I tried my ex-husband and he swore he had already mailed me a child support payment, so I thought I could borrow the money and return it to you this morning. I would have told you what I had done. I wasn't just going to try to sneak the money back, you know?"

"I know, and I wouldn't have minded." He allowed himself to kiss her hair. "If you had put the money back I would have called it fair and square."

"But then everything went wrong. My jerk of an ex-husband flaked out on me. No surprise there." She shifted in his arms, an unwise move given his state of mind. "Your boss did a spot audit. And my parents were also out of town, in Hawaii actually, so I couldn't even get help from them."

"So you were stuck," he whispered against her hair. "But you knew how I felt about you as my secretary. You knew I'd stand behind you. Are you sure you couldn't wait until Monday? That seems strange."

"That's how I felt but I've never bought a home before," she said slowly. "I would have let the home go but Kelsey, my daughter, she loved the house. It has a perfect yard for a dog, and it's close to the homes of two of her best friends from school."

"It's close to here too," Martin pointed out. "You could bring Kelsey over on weekends to swim and ride."

"I could have. Now I'll lose the house." She sounded

defeated.

"Nonsense," he said firmly, "we'll figure it out."

"What do you mean?" Sandy asked, her eyes filled with hope.

"Well first, we'll get Bob from legal to help you two ways. He should look over your contract with the real estate agent and find out why they had to have the money so precipitously. And next, we'll have dear old Bob represent you since you work within the legal system, to get your back child support from the flaky jerk."

"And what else can I do?" Sandy asked, hope returning to her face.

"You let me cover the money you need to keep the house until your full wages are restored. And you keep very quiet about it so Mr. Smithson never guesses."

"You can't mean?" she asked daring to hope.

"Why not? You'll pay me back, in fact you'll probably even insist on paying me interest."

"You'd better believe it, Boss."

"How's your butt doing?" Martin asked suddenly. "Does it hurt too badly?"

She was surprised to realize that it was feeling a lot better already. "It's fine, it's hot and stings, but the worst of the pain has already started to fade." She had stopped crying and smiled at him, a rueful smile. "Thanks."

"For the whipping?" He was surprised.

"For the kindness. For the offer to help me. And especially for the stiff drinks, and for trying to make this absurd situation as normal and polite as possible. Thanks even for giving me the benefit of your past experience as the victim, it helped." She meant it.

"But how about the whipping? I did the best job I could! It was some of my best torture ever!" he said, teasing her. "I've heard that some girls get turned on by it."

"Do they now?" Sandy blushed and dropped her eyes. "Do they indeed?"

"And you were wet," he said firmly.

"And you are hard now," she shot back.

She fell silent for several moments as she rested against him, then her eyes shot open and she shifted herself up to meet his eyes. "Ride?"

"What?" Damn, he'd hoped she'd forgotten that.

"You said Kelsey could come over to ride." Sandy's eyes flashed. "You have horses out back?"

"I own three horses in the barn back there, and I have a gentle pony for when my niece comes over. Jojo could use the exercise. Would Kelsey like to come over and ride him sometimes?" he invited. "And of course she could also go swimming."

"You have horses out back?" she repeated.

He had to try. "So?"

"So I'll bet you already have a riding crop." It was an accusation.

"Of course," he admitted, smiling widely. "So what?"

"So you had me stop to buy one just... " she stopped, speechless.

"To add to your humiliation," he admitted. "My father always made me go get something to beat me with. I usually had to cut a switch. It made the punishment worse."

"And standing facing the wall?" She asked.

"That too," he admitted.

"And picking out a heavy crop, not a thin one?" She had to ask.

"That sounds ominous but it really wasn't. Thin crops hurt more since they seem to cut with a sharper pain." He grinned, "So I was trying to be nice."

"Gee, thanks."

"Think nothing of it."

"About Kelsey riding?" Martin prodded.

"Are you kidding? I think she'd love it! Are you sure it's all right?"

"Yes, I really want you and your daughter to come over to ride and swim when you can."

"We will. Thanks. I think I'd better go home now." She handed her glass to him, "It's been, ah... " She stopped, at a loss

177

for words.

Sandy sighed, "It's been swell, but I'd better get dressed and go home."

"You should stay," Martin decided. "Not for sex, but you've had several drinks and you're upset and exhausted, at least emotionally."

"But I have work tomorrow," she grimaced, "and Mr. Smithson."

"So we'll set the alarm a little early and you can go home and change." Martin coaxed, "I could use some company tonight myself."

"I heard you say something about the weekend, that you were distracted," she asked with concern. "Martin, is everything all right?"

"Yes, it is now," Martin said slowly. "But my father was admitted to the hospital Thursday night. They thought he had a heart attack, but it was a false alarm. Indigestion and heartburn. They were doing tests all weekend." Martin grinned, "So far the one thing they're sure of is that he has a good heart."

"So that's a good thing, right?" Sandy asked.

"You didn't have to spend the weekend with my mother. I love her but she gets so worked up over every little detail." He paused choosing his words. "She seemed almost, hmm, disappointed that it wasn't worse."

"I know the type. It's not that exactly but she builds up her fears so much that she can't let go of them when she finds out there's nothing to fear." Sandy said, "Just give her time to regain her balance. I bet she takes pride in being the backbone of the family"

"She's does."

"I'm getting tired. Do you really want me to stay?" she asked.

"Yes, I do." He helped her up. "I'll show you to your room. Unless you want to sleep with me? No sex."

"With you?" She grinned, "No sex? I wonder which one of us will get the least sleep." She turned serious, "Martin, we could, I mean… "

"We will, and soon. Thank God, it's beginning to seem inevitable, but not tonight." Martin kissed her gently, the first time he had ever kissed her on the lips. "Stay."

"Like I had such a good time, I'd want to stay," she muttered under her breath.

Martin pretended not to hear, "What?"

"Nothing."

"I just hope you weren't insulting my dinner or my hospitality." He teased, "I take my entertaining seriously."

Sandy didn't reply but there was a ghost of a smile, a rueful smile, curving her lips.

Hand in hand they went up to his bedroom. Her clothes were still sitting on the coffee table, forgotten. He gave her one of his soft T-shirts to sleep in, and they got into bed. He kissed her gently goodnight and fell asleep with her in his arms. Or at least he tried. The next morning he woke her with a kiss, this time a real kiss. There was nothing gentle or comforting about it. It was hot, and wild, and wonderful. Sandy, sensible as always, jumped out of bed, showered quickly, dressed and left.

Martin laid back in the bed and thought about the night, the pleasure of seeing Sandy's naked bottom. How round and firm it was. How it seemed to come alive under his hand. How hot and pink it got with only the use of his hand. How red and hot it got under the force of the riding crop. The bruises and welts caused by the belt. He thought of the exquisite joy of holding her, comforting her and cuddling her afterwards. He spent a long time thinking of sleeping with Sandy. Just sleeping. How much more pleasure it would be to stay awake with her? In spite of getting up early, he was almost late for work.

Sandy got to the office first. She ran into Mr. Smithson's secretary, Phyllis, in the lounge while she was getting coffee.

"Good morning," she said without meeting Phyllis' eyes.

"Don't be embarrassed," Phyllis said softly, "Mr. Smithson told me about it. Are you all right?" At Sandy's nod she continued, "As if you would steal. They knew you were only borrowing but those men had to be macho about it. Just an excuse to spank you,

179

you know. It had Rob… I mean Mr. Smithson all worked up yesterday. He'll be randy as a goat again today too. I know I'll wind up getting spanked."

"Really?" Sandy couldn't picture the older man being randy.

"He likes it." Phyllis looked around before confiding with a wide grin, "He takes me over his knees at least once a week. We spend a lot of time together on the sofa too."

Sandy stared at her speechless.

"Oh honey, if you could see your face," Phyllis laughed. "That's not much of a secret. You want to know a real secret? Remember the company policy against married couples working together? Robert and I have been secretly married for almost ten years. And if you play your cards right with Martin, you could be a very happy woman."

"Martin and me?" Sandy was surprised. It was her dearest dream but she thought she had hidden it.

"Why do you think Robert kept insisting Martin spank you?" Phyllis grinned, "It's a hell of an icebreaker, isn't it?" Laughing, she left the lounge and returned to her office.

When Sandy got back to her office, Martin asked her to show him her marks. He was surprised that they had faded so much, but he still called Mr. Smithson to come and inspect the damage.

Mr. Smithson came into Martin's office, the ever present Phyllis at his side. "Call her in, I want to see the marks," he said. "I brought Phyllis along so she'd be less embarrassed."

Martin called Sandy, who was ready. She came in the office and stood there without a word.

"Raise your skirt and show Mr. Smithson your marks," Martin instructed.

With her back to Mr. Smithson, she did as ordered. Because she knew what was coming, she had worn no underwear or panties. Mr. Smithson looked at her bottom and even gently touched a small bruise. He looked over at his secret wife and winked.

"It's an exquisite bottom, my dear. But it's not quite marked enough. Please lean across Martin's desk and let him give you just a taste more," the old man said. "A dozen? Well laid on, should do it."

Martin had brought the crop with him just in case, and ordered a blushing Sandy to bend over the desk. She put herself in the required position, her skirt tucked under her, and waited for the first cut of the crop. CRACK! She gasped and flinched. CRACK! CRACK! CRACK! Her gasps became little cries.

"Can I give her the last two?" Mr. Smithson asked gleefully.

At Sandy's nod, Martin handed Mr. Smithson the riding crop. He gave the last two without as much force as Martin, but instead of trying to avoid the other stripes, he aimed for them. He lightly rubbed the crop at the spot he was aiming for, just to let her know where it was coming, but not when. CRACK! He truly enjoyed her gasp of pain. He also made her wait for the cut until her nerves were stretched to the breaking point. CRACK!

"Come along Phyllis, my dear," he said without hiding his arousal. "We have something to take care of in our own office."

"Yes dear, I mean sir," Phyllis grinned as she left the office.

Mr. Smithson had taken the riding crop. As the old man left, he leaned over and whispered something in Martin's ear that made the younger man blush.

Mr. Smithson had whispered, "That was great! I know she got it hard enough last night but I couldn't resist. Now I'm going to go put this erection to use on my own little darling. I can guess who's going to have to help you use yours."

Martin locked the door behind the old man. Martin walked over to stand behind Sandy, who was showing no sign of getting up from the desk. She heard, as she had the night before, the silky whisper of a belt coming free of its belt loops. Then the unmistakable sound of a zipper. She waited, seeming patient, but actually eager for the invasion of his hard cock into her body. It was rough, wild and primal. It was glorious! They both came in a frenzy.

He helped her to the sofa and brought out a cool, wet washcloth for her sore behind.

"How are you?" he asked, suddenly feeling more than a little guilty as he realized that he had just taken her without any concern about whether or not she wanted him. He stroked her hair gently as she lay there and recovered.

"I feel great!" She reached up and kissed him passionately.

"Even though I just raped you?" He felt more than a little guilty for the last part.

"It wasn't rape." She smiled at him. "Did I say no at any time? In any way? Did I even try to move when I heard you unzip your pants?" She gazed up at him, "From now on. I don't think I will ever say no to you."

"That's good because I'd probably hate prison."

"Then it's a good thing I was as eager as you were," Sandy said dryly.

"Could you be that eager again? Now?" He lowered his mouth almost to hers.

"Well, it shoots the hell out of office decorum, but who cares?" Those were the last words she spoke for a long, long time.

Afterwards as they lay together cuddling, Martin mused, "What do you bet Mr. Smithson's afternoon is not all that different from ours? He took our riding crop, you know."

"That's a sure thing." Sandy confessed, "Phyllis told me this morning he was looking forward to today. I hope she enjoys the crop."

"She told you he spanks her? And that they're lovers?" Martin was surprised.

"She told me more than that." Sandy was smug, "They've been secretly married almost ten years."

"You do realize that old Mr. Smithson knew I had whipped you enough last night? He just wanted to watch and get turned on." He lowered himself onto the sofa. "Too sore?"

"Never, but I want you to know one thing. I wanted you to make love to me even before this happened, and before the spanking," she told him, reaching up for him. "And I'd have to admit, maybe old Mr. Smithson isn't so old after all." That was the last coherent thing either of them said for several long minutes.

"You could have told me that you wanted us to make love,"

Martin said as they cuddled together in the afterglow. "I wasn't sure you even liked me." He kissed her gently on her brow and nose, before moving on to her lovely mouth. "I'm always willing to work hard to try to keep my employees happy." And he did just that from that day on, until the day she quit to become his wife.

Good old riding crops, so useful aren't they? And to think – I wasted them on horses for sixteen years! Spurs can be kinky too. Last night, I finally tied him up. I've spanked him a little but I've always refused to really beat him. Last night I was merciless! Now he wants revenge, so I'll probably spend Sunday night on my stomach!

Author's Note

I'll admit it! I am not above a bit of self-promotion. I put a couple of small excerpts from two other books in here, just as a sample. The scenes with Beauty being spanked by the Beast are from *The Heart of the Beast*. This is more of a romance novel than a purely spanking story, but it has a few spankings in it.

I also put in a scene from my full length spanking novel, *The Paddle Club*. Several of the characters first introduced in these stories also become members of The Paddle Club, and you can read more about them there.

www.ingramcontent.com/pod-product-compliance
Lightning Source LLC
Chambersburg PA
CBHW030505260626
47157CB00005B/1656